MW01487766

THE GIRL AND THE CLOCKWORK CONSPIRACY

NIKKI McCORMACK

ISBN: 0-9963196-2-X
ISBN-13: 978-0-9963196-2-1
First Edition 2015

Published by
Elysium Books
Seattle, WA

All rights reserved. No part of this publication may be copied or reproduced in any format, by any means, electronic or otherwise, without prior consent from the copyright owner and publisher of this book.

This is a work of fiction. All characters, names, places and events are the product of the author's imagination or are used fictitiously.

Copyright © 2015 Nikki McCormack

Written by Nikki McCormack (https://nikkimccormack.com/)
Cover Design by Raquel Neira (http://kellieart.deviantart.com/)
Photography by Michael McCormack
Costuming by Ann Forseth (https://www.etsy.com/shop/RomanyRapture)
Exquisite Cat Model - Koneko
Interior Design by Brian C. Short

•

In loving memory of my dad, Max.
Thank you for always telling me you believed in me.

•

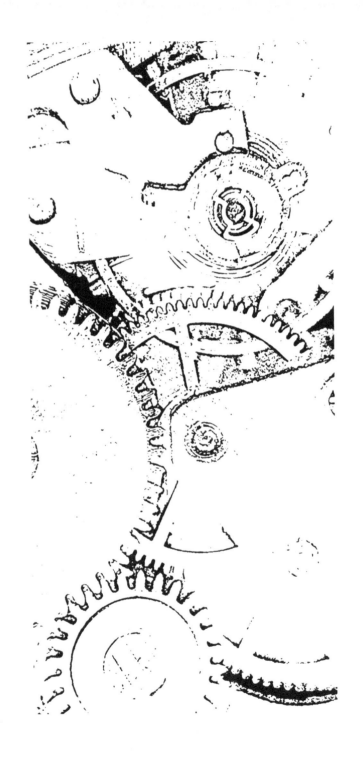

The street was quiet. Too quiet for London at night. The steady dripping of water from a recent rain the only sound. A special kind of unnatural silence lurked in the darkest corners, the kind that promised to line an undertaker's pockets with coin. Detective Emeraude had been around enough to know that silence all too well. It made her skin crawl, triggering the urge to turn back. It was her job to keep going, taking heed of that instinctive warning only in an increase of caution.

"Why're we here, Em?"

She scowled over her shoulder at the stocky man in the bowler cap and put a finger to her lips for silence. Amos stared back at her, small cynical eyes black beads in the darkness. He didn't take the hint.

"We're gettin' paid for this, right? This is somehow going to help us figure out where Mr. Bricker's wife's been spending her evenings?"

To hell with Mr. Bricker and his roaming wife. She gave Amos another warning look.

"Do you even care about the case we are gettin' paid for?" he demanded with a little too much insight.

She looked up at Rueben, seeking support for her cause. The tall Texan offered nothing back. His lazy southern drawl gained physical manifestation in the careless hunch of his shoulders and the bored wandering of his gaze. He didn't agree with her preoccupation

1

either, but he wasn't the type to trouble himself with arguments. Even after three years working together, she still wasn't sure what type he was.

"I have to know why Commissioner Henderson was paying a covert nocturnal visit to Mr. Folesworth." She peered into the dark, watching the shadow-cloaked gentleman striding along, casting furtive glances over his shoulder. That looked suspicious enough, but he had also avoided brighter, busier—and consequently safer—streets since leaving Lucian Folesworth's flat at the top of the Airship Tower. She couldn't see the two men being old chums given the way Lucian's political and financial support of the Literati contributed to the dissolution of the City of London Police and the ousting of the Metropolitan Police Service from many of the London outskirts. The Bobbies no longer had enough funding or political influence in London to fight off the expanding jurisdiction of the Literati's new police force.

"Why we still got our noses in Mr. Folesworth's business? We did the job his brother was paying us for."

This time she ignored Amos. Something about the Folesworth case didn't add up in her head. The mystery of who murdered Lucian's wife and child had wrapped up neatly. Too neatly, perhaps. The killer, Lucian's late business partner Joel Jacard, sat in jail awaiting trial and the supposedly wrongly accused Pirates had returned to their normal lives, cleared of guilt.

That last part peeved her. Damned Pirates danced around the law, claiming to fight for the rights of the common man and getting innocent people hurt or killed more often than not in the process. Maybe Captain Garret and his bunch weren't guilty of *that* crime, but they were certain to bring someone to harm in the name of their misguided subversions if they hadn't already. Still, she didn't think it was the Pirates and street rats getting off scot-free at the end of the case that left her with a bad taste in her mouth. It felt like they were missing something, some deeper subterfuge below the surface, and her instincts were rarely far off.

Except with Maeko.

Em ground her teeth and brushed the thought aside. She crept ahead, sticking to the darkest shadows and trying to keep up with the quick pace set by the MPS commissioner without making enough noise to draw attention. Where was he going now? And why all the secrecy? He'd looked smug coming out of the Airship Tower. What did that mean? What was Lucian Folesworth up to?

The commissioner turned down another dark street, disappearing around the side of a building. Three shots rang out in the night, each one setting off a blast of adrenalin in her. Em sprinted for the corner, drawing the gun out of her shoulder holster. Amos and Rueben kept close behind. The second she passed the edge of the building, another shot fired and she dove for the ground, landing beside the still body of the commissioner. Whoever the shooter was, they weren't looking to leave any witnesses.

"Get back!" she shouted.

Amos and Reuben obeyed, shrinking back behind the corner of the building. She stayed down alongside the commissioner, the cold damp of the wet street soaking through her clothes. The commissioner's blank eyes stared up into a dark, soot black sky. A bullet hole in his forehead seeped red. The shooter didn't fire again. Either they didn't have a good angle or they had decided to make a run for it. She didn't hear footsteps to indicate the latter, but the gunshots would draw more attention soon. Whoever had done the deed couldn't be happy about sticking around.

Two more gunshots split the night. The first hit the corner of the building Amos and Rueben hid behind, sending out a spray of mortar. The second hit a puddle behind her, splashing muddy water on the back of her head and neck. The side of her neck started to sting.

Warning shots. That likely meant they were about to make a run for it. She tensed, holding her breath to listen.

There! Up the street, she heard the sound of someone running and surged to her feet to give chase. Rueben was already out and sprinting. She glanced back and gestured at the commissioner. Amos hurried to the body to stand watch.

Tall as he was, Rueben had a slow southern drawl to his run too. By the time they turned onto the cross street the killer had darted down, she was sprinting alongside him, cool night air spreading icy fingers along her damp side. She spotted a figure running almost a block ahead of them. Average height, lean build, average dress. Easily one of hundreds of men in the city. The type she'd have a hard time tracking down if she didn't get more to work with.

More shots rang out, bullets firing down from the top of a nearby building. Rueben grunted. They both veered to the near side and ducked behind a pile of bricks next to a building under repair. The killer wasn't alone. She peeked out to see their quarry turn down the next street, but she didn't dare give chase now. The rooftop shooter had too good an angle, and he might not be the only one up there.

Rueben crouched down, his right hand clasped tight around his left bicep.

"You hit?"

"Seems so."

She almost grinned at the pained drawl. Did nothing ever get him worked up? "How bad?"

He shrugged, his long face drawn in a tight grimace. Em leaned out as far as she dared and peered up at the roof. A figure stood above, staring into the dark street. Her pistol didn't have enough range to make that distance, but whatever he was firing clearly did. He wore a long jacket full of holes she could see dark grey sky through when he moved and a western style hat with a warped brim. One forearm was thick and bulky, wrapped in a cast perhaps. When he moved, he did so with a significant limp, leaning his whole body to lift his left leg. A hip injury of some kind?

Her smile wasn't kind. Here was someone she could hunt down.

Raised voices reached them from the street they'd just left. The shooter on the rooftop retreated from sight, moving with considerable speed in spite of the limp. Time to get Reuben's arm tended and explain things to the local Lit patrol before they arrested Amos. Em holstered her gun and touched the stinging side of her neck. Her fingers came away sticky with blood. She shuddered. That shot had come a little too close and now her suspects were getting away. She had one distinctive suspect though and a few leads, including a former street rat who might have inside information regarding one part of this mystery.

Em ran a hand through her hair, realizing after she did so that she had most certainly smeared blood in it. She frowned.

It was going to be a long night.

Maeko lay petting Macak who curled against her side, his head on her shoulder. His purr could wake the dead and he snored too. It kept her up sometimes. It didn't matter though. She wouldn't give him up for anything in the world. His furry warmth made the big comfortable bed less intimidating and helped her ignore the selection of dolls staring at her from the dresser. They made her skin crawl. Not because their blank eyes were creepy, though they were, but because she feared damaging them anytime she got near the dresser.

Lucian had his late daughter's clothing removed from the room and stored a few days after he brought Maeko into the house. Why he hadn't removed the toys as well was beyond her. She was too old for most of them, though the little jeweled clockwork elephant that had been on the vanity fascinated her. Lucian said he made it himself and she longed to wind it up, but it felt like an intrusion upon the deceased girl's memory to do so. To fight temptation, she'd tucked it away in a drawer where it wouldn't come to harm. If they had fit, the dreadful dolls would be there too.

The door swept open and a young woman dressed in a fine, if rather simple, tan dress stormed in, brown tresses neatly bundled up on the back of her head under a bonnet. "Still in bed, Miss? Mr. Folesworth is in a sour mood this morning. He won't be pleased with your indolence."

Maeko groaned, not because of the accusation of slothfulness, the thought of her new guardian being in a poor temper, or even the nasty tone reminding her how the housemaid felt about serving someone of her objectionable origins. No, the sound of suffering was inspired by the ominous rustling of the dress Constance laid on the bed before walking over to sweep open the curtains, letting in the dingy light of a gray morning sky.

"Why can't I wear proper clothes once in a while?"

Constance pursed her lips and walked around to pick up the blue dress. "We've been over this a hundred times, Miss. This is proper clothing for a young lady."

"That explains the ongoing confusion then. A lady I'm not."

Constance lowered her voice to a hiss. "Ungrateful scamp. Don't you think I know that? Would you spit on Mr. Folesworth's generosity?"

Maeko disregarded the frosty outburst and kissed Macak on the head where the white and black fur intersected in a peak above his eyes, earning a disgusted scowl from Constance. She slid out of bed then and the cat meowed protest, curling one foreleg over his face.

The housemaid turned away with a gasp. "You know you're supposed to wear night clothes to bed."

Bother. If she had her usual threadbare togs and a blanket full of holes, she would be been fine. "I try, but they're too hot with those covers. I don't see how anyone sleeps buried under all that soft squishy warm stuff."

"Most don't sleep with a nasty old cat for starters."

Maeko tossed a smile over her shoulder at Macak. "Their loss."

Constance huffed and resumed tidying the layers of the dress.

Maeko wiped away the night sweat with a damp cloth using the dreadful perfumed water in the basin on the vanity then dug out the 'proper' undergarments. She caught Constance staring at the healing scar on her shoulder, a disgusted grimace frozen on her face, and turned away. The puncture from Joel's sedative dart had itched like mad for a while, but the scar there was barely noticeable now. The knife wound in her shoulder from her encounter with the murderer she called Hatchet-face had also healed well enough, though the remaining scar wasn't pretty.

The puncture wound from the large sliver that lodged in her forearm when the Literati officer threw her into the crates also formed an angry scar, a constant reminder of Chaff who had pulled the chunk of wood out rather indelicately. He never was one to drag feet about things that needed doing. She might have been annoyed with his rough handling, but he had looked so worried and had even said her name right when he saw her there on the floor of the warehouse. How could she be upset with him?

A smile curved her lips. She hadn't seen him since that night over a month ago, him or Ash, and perhaps the latter was for the best, but she missed them both. Now that her wounds were healed enough not to require so much attention, she itched to get out of the flat and pay some visits.

Constance helped her dress and arranged her short hair as best she could under a small hat with trimmings of blue ribbon. Maeko glanced at the full-length mirror in the corner. No one was going to mistake her for a boy in this silly getup. Why did all dresses have to have frills and lace? They had lace at the cuffs and lace on the bodice and sometimes more lace on the skirts amidst frills and pleats. Worse yet, the ridiculous bustles in the back added to the already burdensome weight of all that fabric. Then there were the corsets. Men who feared their women running away must have designed the hateful things. One couldn't breathe well enough in the fool contraptions to run anywhere and they had rather the opposite effect of the wrappings she'd used on the streets to hide her breasts. She yearned for the tattered boys' clothes she used to wear.

Constance completed the miserable ensemble by helping her into a pair of short-heeled lacey cream boots. Another accessory clearly intended to keep women from wandering astray.

What I wouldn't give for a nice sludgy puddle to give them a bit of character.

Maeko walked from the room with small careful steps, fearful of stepping on the hem of the skirt or rolling an ankle in the insufferable heels. The whir and click of gears in Macak's clockwork leg followed her down the hall.

Lucian sat on the settee in the front room, elbows on his knees and his head in his hands. She hadn't seen a genuine smile on his face since the day she met him, before she told him of the murder of his wife and daughter. Sleeping in his daughter's old room didn't make her feel any better about that, but he insisted on providing her a better life in exchange for saving his. How could a street rat say no to an offer like that from the owner of the biggest company in London?

She moved close and skimmed the newspaper sitting on the table in front of him. The headline read: COMMISSIONER HENDERSON FOUND DEAD OF MULTIPLE GUNSHOT WOUNDS.

Mr. Henderson, the man who had visited last night. He was—had been—Commissioner of the Metropolitan Police Service that was driven out of London proper a few years prior by the Literati and replaced with their own police force. Lucian had sent her to bed when he arrived. She'd even obeyed, several hours later after finding a dark corner from which to listen in for a while to discover the purpose of his visit. If anyone else knew the reasons for that visit, then it was highly likely that the man's murder was connected. No wonder Lucian was in a sour mood.

She chewed on her lip. Should she say something or would it be better to give him time alone?

"Mr. Folesworth." Constance entered the room, giving Maeko a sharp look as if her standing there had been improper somehow.

Lucian lifted his head. Dark hair stuck out in disarray around his narrow face, misery casting deeper shadows under his eyes now than it had the night before, if that were possible. He glanced up at Maeko. His moustache wanted trimming.

She managed a tiny pseudo-curtsy in the hope of starting the day on his good side. "Can I help with something, Mr. Folesworth?"

"Lucian, Maeko. You may call me Lucian in private." He gave her a sad smile, an expression more depressing than his typical tight-lipped frown. "I was going to take you to town and get more proper attire for you today, but I'm afraid I have other affairs I must attend to."

Go to town and get out of this sorrow-filled flat? Yes, please. "I could go alone. I know my way around the city."

He shook his head. "I'm sure you know the city better than I do, but a decent young lady does not go about without a chaperone and I'd wager a fair sum that you don't know how to shop for proper dresses."

Bloody proper everything! She took a deep breath and glanced at the housemaid. Going out in bothersome company was better than not going out at all. "Constance does."

Constance held her hands up and took a step back. "Oh no, Sir. I've got to clean the silver and help Margaret prepare for supper tonight and...and I just don't have time, Sir."

Prepare for supper? That sounded ominous. Were they having company?

Lucian smoothed his moustache and stared down at the paper then he shook his head. "You'd like to get out of the flat I imagine, Maeko."

When he looked at her, Maeko gave him that pleading look that so often earned her what she wanted. His sad smile brightened a fraction.

"Maybe next week we can arrange a visit with your mother. For today, I think Miss Schutz can handle things here. Miss Foster will go with you to help you select some dresses." Constance stared hard at her shoes and Maeko could see muscles in her jaw jump as she ground her teeth. Lucian didn't notice or perhaps he simply didn't care how the maid felt about it. "I'll have my coach take you two over to my wife's tailor on Regent Street."

"My mates don't spend time around there."

Lucian placed a hand on her shoulder. "I'm sorry, Maeko. I think it might be best if you avoided your former companions under the circumstances. You might find those relationships strained by your change in status. I'm sure you can understand that."

She bit back a rising protest and nodded. Some of them might treat her differently, but Chaff wouldn't, would he?

"It is better this way. I'll give you money for food and send a note with Miss Foster to put the dresses on my bill. Please, while you are out in public, do try to remember that you are dressed like a lady."

What did that mean? "Yes, Sir." Macak jumped up on the end table next to her and she met his big bright eyes. "Can I take Macak along?"

"The cat stays in the house where he's safe."

That worked brilliantly for your wife and daughter. She winced, glad she wasn't fool enough to say such a thing out loud. "He could stay in the coach."

"Absolutely not. He's not a dog, Maeko."

"He's probably smarter than one." She scratched the cat under his chin. "Aren't you?"

Lucian's look was unyielding.

She relented. "Yes, Sir." Poor Macak. No adventures for him, at least not when Lucian was watching.

Before they even left the building, it became apparent that this wasn't going to be her usual jaunt in the city. A month spent healing in Lucian's high-class flat had transformed her world, or rather, had transformed her in the eyes of her world. The lift operator, the desk attendant, and the four guards–their numbers increased after the murder of Lucian's family–all greeted her and jumped to offer assistance. They called her miss and tipped their hats instead of threatening to run her in to the Lits as they would have in her former street togs. It was more insulting than flattering.

The driver offered her a hand up into Lucian's private steamcoach, a luxurious bit of highbrow machinery that would carry them into town with Lucian's instructions. One more thing standing between her and any impromptu side trips around the city. True to the rumors, the high-end coaches did have soft velvet seats and a small polished wood beverage cabinet installed in the center of the front seat. Comfortable as it was, the plush accommodations made her feel uneasy and conspicuous when they climbed out by the tailors on Regent Street to engage in the ridiculous business of buying dresses. Any decent pickpocket would be watching who stepped out of the fancy coach in search of a lucrative mark. She would have been.

The shop they entered smelled of fresh flowers and tea. The tailor was a tall man with a high brow and a long narrow nose. After a brief exchange in which her lack of knowledge became readily apparent, he wrinkled his long nose and began to speak exclusively with Constance who excused Maeko's inexperience by explaining that she was Japanese, which was only half true, but it appeared to appease the tailor. She was more than happy to let Constance deal with the stuffy old codger.

The process of letting a shop assistant take her measurements went by fast. Then they began the tedious work of selecting fabrics and patterns. The tailor and Constance dove into that with a passion Maeko couldn't pretend to share, which gave her the opening she needed.

"Const... Miss Foster?"

"Yes, Miss?"

Maeko smiled and asked in her sweetest tone, "Since you're far more experienced at this, would you be so kind as to select materials and styles for me while I take a quick look at a few things in the hat shop down the street?"

The young maid's brows pinched in consternation and she threw a nervous glance at the door as if Maeko had already slipped away. "I don't know, Miss. I don't think—"

"I trust you. You have brilliant taste in clothing," Maeko soothed, deliberately misinterpreting her concern.

Constance flushed. "Well, thank you, Miss. You're too kind, but I still don't think—"

"It's settled then." Maeko beamed at them. "I won't be gone long."

Without giving the maid time to sputter out an argument, Maeko marched through the door and started down the street. Lucian would be brassed off when he found out she'd scarpered off on her own, but she had to at least get word to Chaff so he wouldn't wonder what had become of her. Not only that, she wanted to make sure Detective Emeraude hadn't turned him in to the Lits after they parted ways the night she took Lucian's former business partner, Joel, into custody for the abduction of Lucian and murder of his wife and daughter. Regent Street wasn't a typical haunt for Chaff's boys, but a few of the better pickpockets and cheats frequented the Covent Garden area. That wasn't far. She could get there and back before Constance had time to ratchet up to a full panic.

For the first time, she wouldn't have to keep an eye out for Literati patrols, but her fine clothing would make it difficult to approach the people she wanted to find. Perhaps she could lure one of them in with a little careless dangling of the lovely coin purse Lucian had given her.

She hadn't gone more than a few yards from the door, however, when she spotted a familiar figure loitering outside of a jewelers shop further down the

14

block. The tall, lean woman dressed in men's clothing turned and nodded to Maeko, a slow, opportunistic smile curving her lips. The detective's presence couldn't be a coincidence and her somewhat predatory smile reminded Maeko how short a time they'd been on peaceful terms with one another.

Steeling herself, Maeko approached the woman. The smell of meat pies from a street vendors cart mixed unfavorably with the stenches of burning coal, sweating horses, and manure from the streets. The combination did nothing to calm the nervous roiling in the pit of her stomach.

"I've been thinking about you, Rat," Em started.

"I don't imagine that's a good thing. I take it you followed me here?"

Em pivoted to stare out into the street, her frosty gaze picking over the people there. Maeko also turned.

How differently they must see the crowd before them. Did Em see a possible criminal in everyone or was her offended sneer reserved solely for the less reputable elements lurking in the crowd? Maeko searched out those individuals as well, habitually assessing them for their threat as rivals or potential as allies in a pinch. From Em's expression, it was clear that the latter possibility didn't cross her mind. What in her past left the unusual woman so full of loathing?

"I did follow you. It wasn't hard in that getup." She raised a severe brow at the fancy coach parked along the street. "I've been thinking a lot about the Folesworth murders and Lucian's abduction and your part in resolving all of that. I believe someone with your skills and connections would be handy to have around in my line of work."

"They would?" Maeko asked, sensing an opportunity in the making. Lucian might not appreciate where she came from, but she couldn't forget that part of her life. She would never be comfortable trying to pass as a refined lady and Em appeared to understand that. Working with the detective might open up new alternatives.

A wealthy toff and his lady on clockwork bicycles trundled elegantly by, weaving their way through traffic amidst horse drawn and steam powered coaches. Popular novelty items among eccentric nobility and wealthy tinkerers, the bicycles were one of the few items of new technology that didn't bear the Clockwork Enterprises brand. A pair of Literati steamcycles rumbled down a cross street and a wave of tension rippled through every horse in sight. Maeko too. A month off the streets wasn't quite enough to remove that deep-rooted fear.

"If you were open to working with me, as an apprentice of sorts, I'd give you a cut of the profits." She looked Maeko up and down, her lip curling with distaste. "And I could arrange for some more appropriate working attire."

They agreed upon that much. Dresses were dreadful awkward things. "Shouldn't you be the apprentice? I did track down Lucian on my own after all."

Em responded with a tight-lipped smile. "Don't push your luck. You withheld information I needed and almost got yourself killed for it. That better not happen again."

Maeko's eyes tracked to a swell whose silk handkerchief had worked halfway out of his pocket. Fences paid good money for such items. Another passer caught her attention, a young woman out with a chaperone whose coin purse dangled loose in her hand as she pointed at something down the street. Easy marks both, but she wasn't here for that.

"You did threaten to shoot me at least once," she defended.

"It's a bad habit of mine."

Maeko glanced up at her. "Shooting people?"

Em shrugged as if they discussed some more harmless inclination, such as a tendency toward heavy drinking or gambling. "Are we doing this, or not? I've got other places to be."

Happily, Maeko no longer appeared to be on Em's list of people who need shooting, at least not at the moment. She spotted out a few more good marks walking the busy streets. Lucian would be furious if she agreed to this. Best not let him find out then.

"You must have had something particular in mind when you came looking for me."

Em nodded. "I believe you may already have some information I need for my current investigation, but we can't talk about it here."

"Where then?"

Em gave a nod and a quick wave to someone down the street. A few seconds later, the familiar worn coach drawn by two soot-darkened white horses pulled away from the curb and started towards them, weaving through the heavy traffic. Em glanced at Maeko as the coach pulled up in front of them. "How *did* you find Lucian?"

"Trade secret." Maeko grinned. "I'll share it when you're ready."

"Have it your way," Em grumbled with a shake of her head before setting a foot on the coach step. "Are you coming?"

Maeko hesitated. "Answer one question first. Did you let Chaff go?"

Em exhaled and gazed into the shadowed interior of the coach for a moment. Maeko waited, refusing to move until she had an answer.

The detective finally met her eyes. "Truth is, I wasn't going to. He's a criminal and a kidsman. He should be locked up. But he's also slippery. He scarpered off while we were still getting Mr. Jacard secured in the back of the Literati coach."

Jammy dodger. Maeko grinned and followed Em into the coach. When she sat, the detective closed the door and knocked on the roof. The coach rolled out into traffic.

Maeko nodded to a bandage on the side of Em's neck. "Shaving injury?"

Em narrowed her eyes, not amused.

Maeko swallowed a giggle and pounced on a passing notion. "This is about Commissioner Henderson, right?"

Em's brows rose in surprise. "I find it hard to believe Mr. Folesworth lets you sit in on his private meetings?"

Then Em knew the Commissioner visited Lucian. Which one of them was she investigating? "He doesn't. I was curious what they were meeting about so I listened in."

Em sat back and crossed her arms. "The man must be daft to bring a corrupt little street rat into his home."

Anger flared, having the odd side effect of making the corset feel more suffocating than ever. "You better be paying well if you expect me to help you while you sit there and insult me."

"Really? How much does your pride cost?"

Maeko grabbed the door handle. She had the door open before Em could react and, if not for the ridiculous clothing, she might have made good her escape. Instead, she stepped on the hem of the dress and would have done a face plant into the street if Em hadn't caught her arm and yanked her back. The detective shoved her down into the seat and slammed the door. Then she sat back and Maeko waited for the mocking laughter in the woman's expression to burst free, but Em wrestled her amusement into submission.

"You're right. If we're going to work together, there should be respect, but it better go both ways." She smirked then. "That'll be easier when you have some sensible clothes on."

Maeko rolled her eyes.

"Back to business then. Why did the commissioner meet with Mr. Folesworth last night?"

"Lucian... Mr. Folesworth I mean," Maeko amended, trying to maintain at least a token degree of proper, "offered the commissioner financial backing to help the Bobbies reclaim their lost jurisdiction and work toward gaining a foothold in the city. It sounded like he was looking to give the Lit's police force a kick in the pants."

"Hm. Trying to reset the power balance." Em leaned forward, resting her elbows on her knees. "He must not trust the Literati at all now."

"Obviously."

Em gave her a warning glower for her haughty tone before continuing. "Then he must also believe there was more to the attempt on his life than simply a jealous business partner. Last night's murder would lend support to that theory, assuming it had anything at all to do with their meeting, which seems likely. Do you know who Mr. Folesworth is leaving Clockwork Enterprises to in his new will?"

"How would I know that?"

"I assumed you would have nosed through his things by now."

Maeko drew in as deep a breath as the corset would allow, calming her temper. "Respect."

"Yes. Sorry. You can see where I..." Em trailed off and pursed her lips for a second, putting out a visible effort to be more polite. "Nevermind. He hasn't taken a new partner, so I'd assume he left the company to his brother, though I can't know that for sure. I need you to find out who his beneficiary is without him knowing about it."

"I see. You scorn my shady past until it's of use to you." Em didn't argue. In fact, she didn't seem at all bothered by the accusation. "Fine, but I expect adequate compensation."

"I'll arrange appropriate clothing as payment for the information today. Meet me at the coffee house on the corner opposite the Airship Tower at three tomorrow. If you have the information about the will, you'll be compensated."

"And if I'm not happy with the rate, it'll be the last you get from me."

"I would expect nothing else. And do let me know about any other interesting information you might come across while you're at it." Em drew the curtain back to peer out then knocked twice on the roof and the coach maneuvered to a stop at the side of the street.

She pushed the door open and Maeko stepped out. They'd come around a few blocks and dropped her one street up from the tailors. Constance stood outside the shop wringing her hands and peering up and down the street. The maid looked on the verge of tears. Maeko started toward her as the coach pulled away.

At least she now knew Em hadn't turned Chaff in to the Lits. Getting in touch with him would have to wait for another day.

She tensed when a couple of Literati officers came around the corner and lowered her gaze. The taller of the two, an older jaded bloke by the name of Officer Tagmet with whom she'd had a few unpleasant encounters, altered his course to intercept her. His partner stopped, only following when Tagmet didn't notice his absence. She kept to her course, heading for Constance.

"Miss Maeko!" Constance spotted her and hurried over.

The officers reached her at the same time. Maeko felt a sinking in her gut, but she forced herself to face them. She had done nothing wrong...today.

The younger officer, Wells, shifted his feet, perhaps recalling the day he'd let her get away when she begged him to, insisting she had information that she had to get to Detective Emeraude. He wouldn't meet her eyes.

Tagmet sneered at her. "See that Wells, this area *is* going to the dogs."

"Sir!" Constance sounded truly offended. "This young lady is the ward of Mr. Lucian Folesworth. I beseech you to keep a civil tongue."

Maeko almost laughed at that, but she held back. The red glow suffusing Tagmet's face was a sweet sight, worthy of a better comeback. She smiled back with sour sweetness, taking confidence from the knowledge that, if they did anything to her, news of it would get back to Lucian through Constance.

"Isn't that funny, Officer Tagmet. When I saw you I thought exactly the same thing."

Tagmet stared at Constance a long moment, his face burning bright with furious disbelief. It took a good minute for him to regain control. He took a menacing step toward Maeko, his hand sinking to his gun. The threating motion was enough to make her shrink back a step.

"You may clean up nice enough, but you're still a rat on the inside and eventually you'll muck this up. When you do, I'll be there." With that, he spun away and stormed off into the crowd.

Wells hesitated a second, looking like he might apologize, then he blew out a quick breath and hurried after his partner.

Constance stared after them, her face gone ashen. In a hushed voice she said, "I feared you'd run off for good."

The hint of disapproval in her tone only added to the bad taste the encounter left in Maeko's mouth. "Feared or hoped?"

Constance drew back, giving her a look of unconvincing dismay. "I don't believe I deserved that. Especially after I selected a lovely dress for you for supper this evening." She held up the package in her arms for emphasis. It smelled disturbingly of flowers and tea.

Supper again. "What is so special about this evening?"

"Mr. Folesworth is having some airship captain and his family over for supper."

Maeko felt a bit faint all of a sudden. "An airship captain?"

"Yes, Captain Garrett, I believe is his name."

Of course it is.

Maeko watched her own eyes in the mirror, noting the alarming way they bulged out when Constance pulled the corset laces.

"Exhale," Constance ordered.

"Must I?"

"Yes."

Maeko blew out a breath and Constance expertly drew out the slack.

How exactly was she supposed to breathe in now? There must be grounds in this for an assault charge. Truly? How did women justify punishing themselves in this manner? It was absolute rubbish. What could be the appeal of a waist that small?

Constance tied the corset off and Maeko turned sideways to the mirror.

It did dramatize her somewhat understated feminine curves. Perhaps it would serve a purpose if she were looking to catch a boy's interest, which she most certainly wasn't.

What would Ash think?

Her cheeks warmed.

Chaff would probably laugh himself to death. How humiliating that would be.

She chewed her lip and faced the mirror again. She put a hand on one hip and cocked it toward the mirror, bending her knee a touch to give the posture a jaunty look.

Not so bad.

What if Chaff didn't laugh? What would she do then?

She remembered the kiss he'd given her before Joel was captured. Her fingers started to rise to her lips. She caught herself before the gesture could draw suspicion from Constance, using the hand instead to brush hair away from her forehead.

"You look lovely, Miss, but might I suggest putting the rest of this on before you head out for supper." Constance gestured to the chemise and many ridiculous layers of fabric that made up the rest of the ensemble.

Maeko flushed and allowed Constance to continue dressing her.

She put a hand to her drawn in waist when the rest of the layers were on, feeling a bit lightheaded. "People actually eat in these things?"

Constance pursed her lips, suppressing the amused smile that tugged at the corners of her mouth and finished arranging layers of the dress. She stepped back and turned her gaze to Maeko's reflection in the long mirror. "There you are, a proper lady. And yes, they eat like ladies should. Sparingly."

Maeko frowned and turned to the mirror again. Lavender was a long way from her favorite color, but the two-tone dress of velvet and taffeta was rather flattering. The young woman in the reflection looked so much like a younger version of her mother, before the attack that left her face covered in scars, that she exhaled a breath of surprise. Very little in her features betrayed the non-Japanese half of her parentage. Just as well, since she never knew who her father was other than that he was apparently a wealthy Literati toff with an affinity for brothels. The shorter black hair that had helped draw less attention to her gender in boys clothing looked disturbingly girlish in the dress with all its ornate accents.

She strode away from the mirror and plopped down on the bed, forced into immaculate posture by corset. Macak hopped up on her shoulders, landing light enough not to cause pain in still tender scar there even with his clockwork leg.

Constance made a small distressed squeak like a rusty door hinge and shooed the cat away.

"He was fine there."

"He'll get fur on the dress."

Maeko stared at the fine fabrics spread over her legs. "I can't go out there like this."

Constance walked to the vanity and picked up a small bottle of perfume. She took out the stopper, sniffed it daintily then nodded. "Why not?"

"I look..." She paused, searching for a word that would capture the moment. The smell from the now approaching perfume bottle made her wrinkle her nose.

"Like a beautiful young lady," Constance prompted.

"Absurd." Maeko sprang up from the bed and side-stepped away from the bottle's stopper Constance held out to her. At least this time she didn't stumble in the heeled boots.

Constance gave her a stern look. "You look beautiful. Now let me put some of this on you." She moved toward Maeko again.

Maeko put her hands up between them and backed away. "No."

Constance stopped and pulled the bottle in close to her chest. She stared wide-eyed at Maeko, her jaw tightening.

"I can only take so much of this proper lady bollocks at one time. If I must go out dressed like this I will not wear the perfume." *What I wouldn't give for a simple pair of trousers.*

Constance stoppered the bottle and smacked it back down on the vanity. "Very well, Miss, but next time—"

"We'll talk about next time when it comes around."

It wasn't much of a victory, but at least it was a victory.

A knock drew their attention to the door. It opened to reveal Lucian standing there, his expression far more stern than morose this time, enhanced by the fresh trim of his moustache and tidied hair. He pinned Maeko with his gaze as he walked into the room. "Please excuse us, Ms. Foster."

Constance curtsied and darted out the door. As if the corset alone weren't bad enough, his look and the maid's reaction to it made Maeko feel a bit short of breath. She forced a smile. Lucian walked around her and stopped by the vanity, gazing solemnly down at it.

"Is something wrong?"

He drew in a heavy breath. "Did you sell it?"

She took a wary step closer. "Sell what?"

He turned to her, eyes brimming with bitter accusation. "My daughter's elephant."

Rage swelled until she felt like a blister ready to burst. Anger narrowed her vision. She fought to rein it in, but that only made the accusation hurt more.

"Why did you bring me here if that's how little you think of me?" He looked taken aback by the vehemence in her reply, but she didn't let him respond. She blinked against the sting of tears. "You know what I am and perhaps that's all I'll ever be to you, but if you believe I would steal your dead daughter's things to sell on the street after you took me in, you're not what I thought you were. The bloody elephant is in the top drawer of the vanity. I put it there because I was afraid of breaking it."

Lucian hung his head. He placed a hand on the drawer handle, but didn't open it. "Maeko, I'm sorry." His long fingers tightened on the handle, knuckles turning white with the tightness of his grip. "She was my little girl." His voice cracked.

You deserve to hurt. Guilt swept in on the heels of that thought. She took another step toward him. "Maybe I shouldn't be staying here. You already helped my mum. That's enough."

He drew in another deep breath. "No. You don't belong on the streets. You should be here. Giving you a better life is the least I can do. I shouldn't have accused like that. I don't know why I didn't ask first."

"Because I'm a pickpocket and a sneak thief," she answered.

"You are a remarkable young woman who suffered a great deal to save a foolish man's life. I brought you here because you are so much more than what your life has led you to."

Am I? She said nothing.

He opened the drawer then and drew the elephant out, cradling it in the palm of his hand. "Go on out. I'll be there in a moment."

She left him there, happy to put the unfortunate encounter behind, and followed the rich aromas of cooked meat and warm bread down the hall. Her mouth immediately began to water. It was a shame she wouldn't be able to eat any of that delicious smelling food with the silly corset squishing her stomach up into her throat.

The arrival of Garrett and his family killed much of her appetite anyway. Captain Garrett's limp from the gunshot wound Em left him with—when she thought him guilty of murdering Lucian's family—was much improved. She hadn't seen Ash, Garrett's eldest son, since he'd held her in the coach on the way to have her injuries tended after they rescued Lucian. She wanted to see him again, but not like this. Not with all the annoying proper etiquette forcing them to greet one another politely and sit quiet over supper. His discreet approving smile when she greeted him didn't help her relax either. Perhaps he meant it as a compliment, but it made her feel self-conscious while she tried to hold up her end of a frivolous chat with Garrett's wife Julia.

Aside from being Garrett's wife, Julia was also a member of his Pirate band, that Maeko had first met in a pub over near Cheapside. The talk of dresses and food didn't seem to suite her temperament either, but perhaps it was simply an attempt at propriety for their host's sake. It was deathly boring and Maeko found herself studying details of the room to stop herself from dwelling on all the mouthwatering food she didn't have space for in her ridiculous attire.

The table laden with its burden of savory selections had ornate carved legs and was polished to the point that she could see her own reflection in the dark wood surface. The chairs had elaborate wrought iron scrollwork set into the backs and the legs were scaled down versions of those on the table. A handsome standing clock at the far end of the room and the fancy curio cabinet full of fine silver dishes and various intricate clockwork devices along the other wall held her attention for a time. That she couldn't forget what those dishes and trinkets would sell for on the street only served as a reminder that she didn't belong here in these fancy rooms wearing fancy clothes.

At the end of dinner, Garret and Lucian retreated to the study to talk business and have a smoke. The rest of them moved into the front sitting room. Julia sat twisting her wedding ring around on her finger and watching her younger son Samuel, his rigid fake leg set off at an odd angle to work around the center table, while he stroked Macak on the settee and made wistful comments about the cat's much more functional prosthesis. Maeko watched from another chair, finding few words to contribute. Ash stood flipping through Lucian's stack of science journals much too fast to be reading anything.

He set the last one down and glanced at Julia. "Mum, can I take Maeko out to see the airship?"

Julia eyed them both and Maeko feared she would insist that she or perhaps Constance accompany them. The dreaded idea of chaperones, another foolish shackle deemed necessary by high society. Then she gave a tiny shrug. "I suppose that would be fine, but don't mess with anything, not even if Jack says you can."

"Thanks." Ash stood and gestured with a jerk of his head toward the door on the far side of the formal dining room that led up to the airship dock.

It took considerable restraint not to leap up and sprint out the door. Maeko made herself walk over and up the short flight of stairs beyond the door with a modicum of dignity if not with grace, trying to show that she was enough of an adult to be trusted alone with Ash. An enclosed guardhouse stood to one side of where they came up. The tower kept that post manned at all hours since the murders. The guard there nodded as they passed, never quite taking his attention away from the newspaper he was reading.

Garrett's airship was the only one anchored there, the same bulky patched up model she had seen landing the first time she visited the Airship Tower in search of Macak's owner, the night she'd found Lucian's wife and daughter dead.

Perhaps someday everything here would stop reminding her of that awful sight.

Warm light shone through the windows of a gondola attached to the underside of the airship. She could see the other two members of the Pirate band inside sitting back and having a chinwag, their feet rested up on the controls and drinks in hand. Their laughter crept out into the night, sounding impossibly far away from within the enclosed space.

Ash hunched his shoulders to the brisk night breeze and she sympathized, wishing she had thought to grab a shawl or something to keep away the chill. At least the breeze had blown away much of the smog, giving them a view of the city with its many gas lamps and houselights glowing, a sparse array of landlocked stars in the darkness.

As curious as she was about the airship, they couldn't talk privately there so she adjusted her course, heading over to the darkest edge of the roof where comforting shadows waited to welcome her. She placed her hands on the rail. So cold. The steel was smooth, like ice under her fingers, sending gooseflesh up her arms. Ash stopped beside her and she could see him watching her from the corner of her eye.

He had made it clear that he cared about her as more than a friend. He would be expecting her to figure out who she wanted to be with, but she hadn't even known Chaff had deeper feelings for her until the moment he kissed her. How could she choose between them when it was all still so new and confusing?

"Is something wrong, Mae?"

At least he pronounced her name right, Ma-eh and not May as Chaff liked to say to get under her skin. And yet, the thought of that teasing lifted her spirits and brought a fleeting smile to her lips. "I'm a little surprised your mum let you come out here alone with me."

"Why?"

"I'm not the type of girl most parents want their sons around."

He took her hand, his gentle pull encouraging her to face him. She gave in, not ready to face him, but not wanting to hurt his feelings by refusing.

"Don't be droll. You've come up in the world and, if it isn't too forward of me to say so, society looks splendid on you."

What to say to that? She met his lovely pale green eyes and darted her gaze away from the open admiration in them. His praise was too forward to be appropriate, but she didn't care much for propriety. She knew what she should say, though the words didn't feel right when she forced them past her lips. "Thank you."

He took a step closer, one warm hand, calloused from working on airships with his father, still held hers, his gorgeous eyes all but glowing in the dim moonlight, his dark hair mussed by the breeze.

Her heart sped up and she flushed, wondering if he could feel the racing pulse through her hand.

His voice was soft when he spoke this time, a deep whisper. "I've been yearning to see you again."

In retrospect, finding the darkest part of the roof might have been a bad choice.

He reached out and placed a hand on her cheek, his touch awkward and uncertain, a slight tremble in his fingers. His gaze dropped to her lips.

What would it be like to kiss him? She started to step closer, drawn by the need and desire in his eyes.

CHAPTER FIVE

Chaff popped into her mind then, the touch of his lips on hers, the way his strong hand felt so sure and confident holding her to him, his perfect scoundrel grin when he'd drawn away from that stolen kiss.

Her cheeks flushed hot and she stepped back from Ash, leaving him leaning in with one hand hanging in the air where her cheek had been. A regretful ache rose in her chest and she pulled her hand away, turning to stare out over the rail again. Ash stood staring at her for a long moment before he too turned to look out over the rail, his fierce gaze tearing into the darkness. In the tension-filled silence that stretched between them, the banter of a couple walking in the street below rose up to the rooftop, the woman's heartfelt laugh shimmering like a star in the dark. How happy they sounded. What dreadful timing they had.

Maeko chewed at her lip.

"It's him, isn't it?"

She glanced at Ash, unable to admit it even though she knew exactly what he meant. "What? Who?"

"It's because of that bloody street rat. You're sweet for him, aren't you."

Maeko turned on him, the comforting boil of defensive anger chasing away pangs of guilt. "I'm not sweet for him. And it would serve you well to remember that I'm no more than a street rat myself." She winced at her own hypocrisy, defending a title she typically regarded as an insult.

"Yes you are," he snapped then swept a hand out to point toward the door that would take them back to Lucian's flat. "You've left that life behind."

"No, I haven't, Ash. Dresses and fancy coaches don't change who a person is. No amount of money will ever erase the fact that I was born in a brothel and spent most of my life on the streets with that *bloody street rat* looking after me—"

"Using you!"

His face flushed with anger now. She imagined hers was much the same. Not a flattering emotion.

"You're wrong. You're wrong about him and you're wrong about me." Her throat tightened and she threw up her hands. "To hell with all this proper bollocks!" She spun away, wavered precariously on her heel a moment before catching her balance, then stalked back to the door. Ash didn't follow. That was almost as much a disappointment as it was a relief. Maybe he was beginning to realize she wasn't worth the trouble.

Confusion made a maelstrom of her thoughts and her vision blurred. She yanked off the boots at the bottom of the stairs, slunk through the kitchen to avoid Julia and Sam in the front room, and hurried down the hall to her borrowed bedroom. She shut the door gently, not wanting to alert the two men in the adjacent study, and flopped down on the bed. The dolls on the dresser stared at her, their perfect little faces and round rosy cheeks made her want to smash them. She rolled onto her side, putting her back to them.

There was a light knock on the door several minutes later. Maeko said nothing, hoping whoever it was might go away. The door opened. Macak jumped up on the bed and trotted over to her, the articulated metal armor of his false leg gleaming when the intruder lit a sconce alongside the door.

"Miss Maeko."

Constance. "Yes."

"Young Mr. Asher said you excused yourself because you weren't feeling well."

Maeko said nothing. Macak licked her hand.

"It's probably the corset. They take some getting used to. Let me help you out of those clothes and I'll make your excuses."

Here at last was a benefit of stuffy society life that she could appreciate. Usually she had to make all her own excuses.

She let Constance help her out of her clothes and changed into the night shift the maid pulled out for her. After Constance turned out the light and left, she sat cross-legged on the bed, listening and petting Macak, waiting for the house to go to sleep so she could begin the work that had nothing to do with proper society or boys. Eventually, she heard the distant hiss of the airship crew releasing air from the ballonets to gain lift. A minute later, the engines kicked in.

A twist of guilt burned like acid in her stomach. Had she turned Ash away because of Chaff or was it that nagging certainty that he would never really understand her? Did he honestly want Maeko the uncivilized street rat or was he more interested in the society lady he expected her to become now that Lucian had taken her in?

Macak meowed, protesting the increasing aggression in her strokes and she eased off, scratching under his chin in apology. His contented feline smile made her grin and she leaned down to plant a kiss on his fuzzy head.

"I've got you now, don't I? What else could I possibly want?"

She curled around the cat and closed her eyes. Sleep toyed with her for a time, drawing her down to a troubled slumber then sending her back toward awareness only to pull her down again. Sometime later, sleep spit her out in an alert state and she slipped off the bed. She grabbed the embroidered satin robe Lucian had loaned her on the way out of the room. It belonged to his late wife and was too long, but at least if she were caught sneaking around she would be decently covered.

The study door at the end of the hall past her room was closed as it always was and for the first time she wondered if Lucian might keep it locked. That would be a bother. Her lock pick tools and the set she'd nicked off Chaff vanished with her old clothing after Lucian took her in. She could find something in the house to work it open with, but that would take time and increase her chances of getting caught.

The door opened when she turned the knob, allaying her concerns. After standing in silence for a count of sixty to listen for sounds of stirring within the flat, she slipped inside. Macak trotted in with her, his clockwork leg whirring and clicking. She shut the door behind him, happy to have a furry accomplice. Taking a chance, she turned up the wall sconce. It would be easier than digging around in the dark and a candle would be a nuisance.

The room was rich with the sweet smoky smell of cigars. Two tall filing cabinets stood along the wall to the left of the door, Lucian's grey coachman hat sitting on top of the nearest one. The far wall held shelves tidily organized with sets of books arranged around more strange clockwork gadgets. Prototypes developed for his business perhaps. His desk sat in the center of the room, a large deep chair behind it suggesting authority and another plush chair sitting opposite that allowed for comfort and long visits. Macak opted for the smaller plush chair to curl up and take a bath in.

As she moved into the room, a figure in the corner caught her eye. A small battered boy made of wood and metal sat on a stool there, painted features faded and scuffed with age. Like Macak's false leg, the fingers and arms were articulated, but unlike the leg, the workmanship was rough and amateurish. The index finger on the right hand had been replaced with one made of inflexible wood and an articulated finger, the original perhaps, hung on a string around the boy's neck. A framed blueprint drawn up in a youth's rough hand hung above the boy with Lucian's name scrawled in the corner. There had to be quite a story behind the boy, but she couldn't ask since that would require admitting that she'd been in the room.

Dragging her attention away from the boy, she tried to decide where he would keep a copy of his will. A quick search through the folders in the big cabinets showed that they were dedicated to patents and ideas for inventions. The ideas were most interesting. A bottom drawer held numerous weapon designs tucked toward the back. In the front of the same drawer hung several folders full of rough sketches for artificial limbs, some of which included ideas for extra functionality such as detachable tools for construction.

It would take hours to look at all the drawings so she dragged herself away from the fascinating selection.

A side table next to the window behind the desk held a selection of alcohols on the lower shelf. Tucked alongside the table was another small cabinet. She knelt down in front of it and began to peruse the folders in there. The third one back held what she wanted. She sat on the floor and started to skim the will. There were plenty of unfamiliar words in the text, but her mother had taught her to read well enough to get the meaning of much of it. The part that puzzled her however was that the document left nearly all of his assets to his late wife and daughter. Wouldn't he have written a new one after their deaths? Maybe there was another one hidden somewhere.

She tucked the will back in place and started a second search through the contents of the cabinet. Macak's soft meow drew her attention. The cat had abandoned his bath and was staring at the door, his tongue still half out of his mouth. Then another sound made her nerves spark to life. Footsteps. She tucked everything back in place and shut the cabinet. There was no escaping now so she leaned against the wall by the window and stared out as if she'd been there for some time, focusing on making her breathing slow and even. Subterfuge was one of her specialties after all and, after the earlier incident with the elephant, he might be hesitant to assume the worst.

The door swung open. Lucian stepped in and stalled in the doorway, staring at her. "What are you doing in my office?"

He continued into the room, walking around behind the desk. She moved around the opposite side, stopping in front of it. Macak jumped up on the desk then bunched and jumped again, landing light on her shoulders. She put a hand up to steady him, though he didn't seem to need it. Facing Lucian with the cat there bolstered her courage.

"I was looking for someplace quiet to think. Sometimes I can't sleep in that room knowing it isn't supposed to be mine."

The muscles in his jaw jumped and he slammed a hand down on the desk. "Nor is this study yours."

She cringed and took a step back. He wasn't in such a forgiving mood after all. "I'm sorry."

He frowned. "Since you're here, I had something to discuss with you. Am I to understand you were on the roof alone with that boy, Asher?"

She shifted her feet back a little more, inching toward the door. It was hard to keep bitterness from her tone. "Yes, Sir."

"You shouldn't have been up there unsupervised. So long as you are living under my roof you need to behave as other proper ladies do, even when—"

She threw up her hands, cutting him off and startling Macak who dug in his claws for balance. The pain sharpened her mind and helped keep her shame at lying to Lucian locked away. "Proper again. I've barely been here a week and already I'm sick to death of trying to be proper for everyone."

She spun around and Macak dug in hard enough to bring tears to her eyes.

"Maeko!"

Run away. Don't give in to him. She stopped in the doorway and rotated slowly around to face him again.

Lucian was staring at the desktop now. "I'm sorry, Maeko. My life has been through such upheaval of late. I'm afraid I often forget how much change you're trying to cope with. Please sit down." He gestured to the chair in front of his desk and sat in the one behind it.

Maeko walked back and sank into the chair, wiping at a tear that streaked down one cheek. Sensing the calming mood, Macak retracted his claws. He began to lick her ear. She put a finger in between his tongue and her ear and he nibbled at it with sharp little teeth.

"I forget you're used to living in a den of boys. None of them ever did anything to you, did they?"

She stared for a moment, puzzled, then recalled Officer Wells asking a similar question about Hatchet-face, the murderer who had helped her escape JAHF the first time. *Oh, that kind of anything.* "No. Chaff would never allow that," she assured him.

"Chaff?"

Daft. She chewed her lip. "He's the one who brought Detective Emeraude to the warehouse to arrest your partner. He taught me how to survive on the streets." *And steal and pick locks. All those things proper girls don't do.*

Lucian nodded. "I remember. I had taken him for one of her hirelings until I saw the way he reacted to you. Has *he* ever done anything to you?"

Her treacherous cheeks grew warm. "No."

"I see." His fingers tapped the desk, his expression one of considerable skepticism.

"I said no."

"Your lips said no, the rest of you said otherwise. I'm inclined to believe the latter."

She started to search for another argument then gave up. Some battles were meant to be lost and the truth would be better than what he might come up with on his own. "It was only a little kiss and only once," she confessed.

"Entirely inappropriate behavior for a young lady. There are proper ways to be courted and proper young men to be courted by." She bristled at that, but held her tongue. "I will see that you are taught both. Until you understand the rules, however, please assume that any unchaperoned contact with young men is improper."

"Yes, Sir."

He opened a drawer and stared into it for several seconds.

Were they done? Could she leave now? She started to get up only to settle back down again when he spoke.

"I can't sleep either, knowing my wife and daughter are gone forever." He drew a cigar out of a case in his drawer and snipped the end off. "Did you and Asher have an argument?"

Her chest tightened. *How did he figure that out?* She could think of nothing to say while he struck a lucifer and rotated the cigar over the flame, puffing at it until it was evenly lit. The big cigar made his narrow face look almost comically small. He held the cigar away from his mouth and gazed at her.

"Asher seems like a nice young man, but there are plenty of nice young men out there. I don't think you should trouble yourself with such things while you're still trying to adjust to this life. You'll have plenty of suitors to choose from when the time comes."

She held back a sigh. How nice it would have been if he would have consented to letting her go find Chaff instead of forcing her to sneak around behind his back. Clearly, it wasn't worth bringing the idea up. He didn't even want her consorting with Ash. Meeting up with Chaff was out of the question. "You're probably right."

He nodded as if the subject were resolved. "Next week I'll have a governess start coming to the house to work with you on your studies."

Bugger! "Yes, Sir."

"You should try to get some sleep. I want you to think of that room as yours now."

With her dolls staring at me? Macak pressed his cold moist nose into her ear and she brushed his face away. "Yes, Sir." The cat continued to ride her shoulders as she stood.

"One more thing." He waited until she met his eyes to continue. "When you go to town with a chaperone the idea is that they go everywhere with you. Running off alone is not conduct befitting a lady."

Oh that. "I understand." She started to turn away and her eyes lit upon the clockwork boy. "What happened to his finger?"

His eyes tracked to the corner and a wistful smile stole across his lips. "That was the first thing Joel and I built together. We were thirteen. It used to sit at a toy piano and play songs."

"That thing could play the piano?"

The smile warmed a little in response to the disbelief in her tone. "Only simple songs. It earned us so much praise from our parents that my brother Thaddeus got jealous and stole one of the fingers."

"Why didn't you fix it?"

He shrugged. "Thaddeus gave the finger back three years later. By then, Joel and I had moved on to much bigger things."

The sorrow in his tone and the slow fade of that wistful smile spoke volumes to the sense of loss he felt at his partner's betrayal. If they'd been friends that long, she imagined it must have been heartbreaking. There wasn't much she could say or do for that.

He turned away from the boy and began to dig in another drawer. "Goodnight, Maeko."

"Goodnight, Sir."

Being stuck in the flat was starting to feel a little like being locked up at JAHF for a third time, although decidedly more comfortable. Lucian had gone to take care of some business at his main factory. The meeting with Garrett had worked to spur him back into his business, which was probably a good step in his recovery and it left Maeko what appeared to be a great opportunity to slip out and meet Em. Only, the first time she reached to open the front door, Margaret stepped into the room with a warning that she shouldn't be heading out alone without the master's approval. After that, both maids developed an extra sense that brought them out to the front room every time she moved toward the door with the intention of leaving.

Maeko tried wandering back to Lucian's office, thinking she might have another look around for a new will, but the moment she turned her attention that way, Margaret appeared and began dusting framed blueprints hung along the hall. Concerned that it might be her actual intent they were sensing, she made an effort to approach the front door without intent. That didn't work either. Constance bustled into the room and began wiping down tables for a third time.

Thwarted, Maeko took to pacing the flat, counting the steps it took to get from one room to another.

Whenever Macak wasn't riding along on her shoulders, he paced along behind, every click of his clockwork leg like a second hand counting down, reminding her that she would be late to her meeting soon.

She developed a pattern, pacing to the study door, to the window in her room, to Lucian's bedroom window, through the kitchen, around the dining room table, across the front sitting room and back to the study door to start over. The route made her cross paths with Constance and Margaret often enough they began to go about their cleaning with pursed lips and harried glowers. A small price to pay for the cruel act of holding her hostage.

Maeko turned into the kitchen on her thirteenth circuit. Constance, preoccupied with cleaning, ran into Maeko this time, letting off a frustrated squeal when she staggered back a few steps.

"Miss Maeko, you need to…" Constance started to snap then trailed off before Maeko's challenging stare.

They faced off for several seconds, Constance with her mouth hanging open at a loss for words and Maeko glaring daggers into her, daring her to complain.

Then Constance smiled with false sweetness. "I have an idea. Mr. Folesworth does love fresh bread with dinner, but we haven't had time to step out today. Would you be a dear and run to the bakery? There's a bit of coin in the box by the journals and I'm sure he wouldn't disapprove of such a brief unchaperoned outing."

The daggers fell away. Could it be that easy? Perhaps Lucian hadn't sufficiently emphasized to them his opinion that she required a chaperone to interact with the world outside the Tower. There was no sense questioning her good fortune. "Brilliant idea! I'll be back in a jiffy." *Or sometime thereafter.*

Maeko spun around, nearly stepping on poor Macak who sprinted down the hall after giving her an indignant look. She went to her room and snatched up a dainty little coin purse from the dresser by the staring dolls, giving them a sour glare on her way out. After collecting some coin from what she had originally assumed to be an ornate snuffbox, she marched to the door.

"Don't be long," Constance called after her in a tone that sounded more as if she wished many varieties of dread misfortune on Maeko so long as it kept her out of their way.

Macak slipped out on her heels and sprang up to wrap himself around her shoulders like a fur scarf. She lifted him off and looked him in the eye.

"I can't take you, mate. Lucian would never forgive me if something happened."

The cat stared back at her then blinked once, slowly. It didn't matter a whit to him what Lucian thought.

Maeko nodded and placed him back on her shoulders. "You're right. It isn't as if we'll be going far."

Down in the lobby the desk attendant, who couldn't seem to decide between looking at her and staring at the cat on her shoulders, inquired if she would be needing transportation. She almost said yes. Oh how she wanted to go find Chaff and visit her regular haunts around Cheapside, but she needed to meet Em. There was an opportunity for a future here that was worth following up on. Chaff would have to wait for yet another day. She declined the offer, stepped on the plate that opened the steam-powered doors, and went outside.

There were always a few steamcoaches kept on retainer for the convenience of Airship Tower residents. Two of these were parked out front bearing familiar brass plaques with Lucian's Clockwork Enterprises brand stamped upon them. An unnerving reminder of the strange fortune she'd found by picking up Macak in a back alley while hiding from a Literati patrol. The resulting adventure had almost gotten her killed more than once, but almost didn't really count. Did it? Life was a peculiar thing. Of course, now she had to put up with itchy lace collars, insensible shoes, and the bothersome restrictions of proper society behavior. Even wealth had its down sides.

Maeko strode down the block, observing the curious way people reacted to her now. As a ragged street rat, they rarely deigned to notice her and, if they did, it was with a disapproving scowl and turned up nose. They still didn't pay her much mind, but those who did gave a polite smile or nod, their eyes widening a touch if they noticed the cat around her shoulders. A couple of blokes even tipped their hats and wished her good morning, calling her miss. It was hard to remember to smile and nod back rather than stare at them dumbfounded.

At the corner, she stopped to wait for an opportunity to cross the busy street, Macak looking left and right as if he too were looking for a break in traffic. She twirled the coin purse on her finger while she watched horse drawn and steampowered coaches pass by. A coach driver shouted at a costermonger who had halted in the street to fiddle with something on his cart. The coster responded with a rude gesture, but he did begin to move again, muttering something under his breath. Big omnibuses trundled along, forcing their way through traffic, while pedestrians and the occasional brave cyclist wove through the press. A noisy Literati steamcycle sped past, startling some of the horses and making Macak tense. Maeko stuck her tongue out at the officer's back, earning a startled glance from a woman walking past.

She gazed after the woman and sighed. More of that improper behavior she was supposed to be unlearning.

A small tug on her finger grabbed her attention and she turned in time to see a boy no older than seven in tattered togs sprinting down the pavement with her coin purse in hand. He hopped on an omnibus that was pulling away and winked back at her as he tucked the purse in his pocket.

Cheeky little jackanapes! She couldn't let him get away with that. Maybe she was high society at the moment, but who knew how long that would last. Nothing good could come of letting a junior pickpocket get the better of her.

Maeko lifted Macak and tucked him under her arm as she hurried back to the attendant in the Airhsip Tower. "Might I take one of those coaches after all?"

"Certainly, Miss." He hailed a coachman loitering by the door.

"Thank you." She hurried back outside with the coachman and pointed down the street at the retreating omnibus. "I need to follow that bus."

The coachman frowned at the heavy traffic, but he opened the door for her, also offering a nod to Macak as she climbed in. "As you wish, Miss."

Taking his task to heart, the coachman worked his way through the press, shouting at those who dared dally in his path. She leaned out the window to watch ahead, keeping an eye on the bus in case the thief disembarked. She wrung her hands, chewing at her lip as they worked their way farther from the Tower. This wasn't the way to please Lucian, nor was it likely to make Em overly happy with her, but she couldn't let the thief go.

The chase led them over to Cheapside and she began to wonder if the little sneak had gotten off without her seeing, then he appeared at the door, leaping off while the bus was still in motion. The conductor shouted after him and he ran.

Skipping the fare.

The steamcoach slowed with traffic and she opened the door, stepping out and almost doing a face plant because of the silly heels. The coachman continued on, unaware of her departure. Just as well. She didn't need him telling anyone where she'd been.

A plaintive meow drew her gaze to the pavement. She snatched up Macak, tucking his clockwork leg against her body to hide it. "Sorry mate, forgot I had help," she murmured, scratching his head.

She followed the boy, keeping enough distance between them so as not to be too obvious about it, though he didn't look concerned. The little rat thought he'd gotten away with it. They turned several more times, moving into poorer streets where the smell of waste still permeated the air despite the advent of sewers. In her fine clothes, she began to get shifty glances from ragged locals and her skin prickled with unease. Still, she focused on her quarry. Ahead of her, the boy paused to look around and she pressed back against the wall of a building behind a listing barrow with a missing wheel. After a hasty survey of the area, the boy ducked between two boards into an old closed up building.

Maeko smiled to herself. She didn't recognize the boy, but she knew the building. It was one of Chaff's primary lurks, down the street from a rowdy gin palace. That meant the boy was working for him. If he expected to lose her now, he was in for a surprise.

She set Macak in through a low opening then ducked between the same two boards nailed over the door only to be caught up halfway through because of the ridiculous layers required to get the proper hang in the skirt. It took a few precious minutes, filled with muttered curses the occasional impatient comment from Macak, to work her way free without seriously damaging the material. As it was, she emerged with several snags that would require repair and difficult explanation.

Inside, she took off her hat and the heeled boots, leaving them next to the entrance. She'd had to navigate the building barefoot several times in her years on the streets and the boots would be too loud on the old wood floors. Not to mention awkward for climbing around debris, something that already promised to be difficult in these clothes.

She gestured ahead. "Let's go find ourselves a rat," she murmured to the cat who dutifully trotted off in the direction the boy had gone.

The smells of dust and mildew filled her nose so she had to fight back a sneeze. The building was a shambles inside. A low cost housing unit that partially burned at one point, though heavy layers of dust and cobwebs in the unused front rooms hid much of the black char, muffling the old burn stench. Many walls and floors in the front rooms had collapsed over time. Macak's precise footsteps didn't stir the debris and she knew where to step to make the least noise and leave the least evidence of her passage.

She didn't have to go far in before she heard the soft chink of coins. Peeking around the corner, she spotted the boy sitting on a chair so thick with grime that it blended with the sickly greenish-brown staining the walls. Stuffing poured out of holes made by nesting rodents. The boy held her purse up and jingled it, grinning to himself. Now that she got a better look, she thought he might be eight, but certainly no older, and the mop of brown hair sticking out from under his worn cap needed a trim.

Macak's ears perked. She didn't try to stop him when he continued into the room. The boy started when the cat entered, his expression switching from relief that it was only a cat to amazement when the clockwork leg came into view. After a few seconds, he grinned and held a hand down to the cat.

Taking advantage of his distraction, she padded into the room. When the boy noticed her, his grin vanished and he crammed the purse in a pocket, springing to his feet. He bolted for the next doorway and Macak leapt up to the back of the chair, settling in to watch the action. Maeko lunged after the boy. The skirt of her dress caught a nail in the floor, pulling her over, but her hand caught his trouser waist and she dragged him down with her. The boy cried out. He twisted around, flailing like a wild animal. She rolled away to dodge a flying fist and ended up on her back in a thick carpeting of dust and rodent droppings. The boy pounced on her and began swinging, striking her in the right eye then the left side of her mouth.

Struggling against the restricting clothes, Maeko finally caught the third flying punch in her hand and sat up, swinging her elbow out like a chicken wing in front of her and landing solid blow to his nose. The boy reeled back, throwing his hands over his nose, and she twisted, bucking him off. She jumped to her feet to the dreadful sound of tearing fabric and poised to go after him again when someone caught her by the arm and swung her around into the wall. The impact stunned her. She sucked in a startled breath, inhaling some of the dust and debris that rained down. A fit of coughing overtook her.

"Who the bloody hell do… May!"

"Ma-eh," she spat, sending a fine spray of red from her bloodied lip onto Chaff's shirt font before falling victim to another fit of coughing.

"Lousy bird bloodied my nose." The boy's voice sounded muffled behind his hands. He was glaring at Maeko over grimy fingers.

Macak, deciding the excitement was over, lay down and started to clean one paw.

Chaff stared at her, a bemused smirk curving his lips and the shine of humor brightening his blue eyes. "I'm not surprised. You're lucky she didn't do worse." He looked her up and down then and the expression darkened. "Are your cogs rusted, Pigeon? What are you doing wandering around here dressed like that? You're lucky some bludger didn't have a go at you."

The coughing fit finally passed. She ignored Chaff's comment and returned the boy's glare. "That miserable scamp nicked my tin."

Chaff lifted one brow. "*He* nicked *your* tin?"

She glowered in silence at the young boy, aware that shame now burned her cheeks like a brand. Yes, the accomplished thief had her purse nicked by a mere boy. Not a proud moment.

Chaff barked a laugh. "That's a fine thing. My star pupil robbed by a new recruit."

"Yeah, well he didn't do so splendid making his getaway. Maybe if his hair wasn't in his eyes he'd have noticed I was tailing him."

Chaff contemplated the boy over his shoulder for a moment then held a hand back to him. The boy tossed him the purse. "Go find Diggs and have him take a look at your nose. And do something about that hair."

With one last hate-filled glare for Maeko, the boy got to his feet and scampered deeper into the ruined building.

Chaff's eyes narrowed in puzzlement as they homed in on Macak then he turned to her and grinned like the charming scoundrel he was. He tossed the purse in his palm, weighing the value of the coin with an experienced hand. "I'll be keeping this to replace those lock picks you nicked off me."

"You can't keep that, Chaff, it ain't mine."

"Isn't." He corrected and reached out to run his fingers through her hair, brushing away bits of debris. Then he took her chin between his thumb and forefinger and tilted her head back a little. "Looks like you've earned yourself a bit of a shiner and a split lip."

He was right about both. She could feel the sting, but as she looked up at him, those things faded before the memory of that kiss he had stolen before she went to save Lucian. A giddy warmth spread through her, making her feel almost as silly as the way she was dressed. She tried to shove the feeling away. "That money belongs to Mr. Folesworth."

He glanced over his shoulder at Macak again, eyes widening as he noticed the metal paw poking out from under the cat. "I've had my boys scouting work houses and orphanages for you. I didn't know the inventor took you in. Blimey Pigeon, when you move up in the world you don't mess around." He tucked the purse in a pocket. "I'm sure he won't miss this scant bit, though I imagine he'll be missing that cat quick enough."

With the money tucked away, he put one hand against the wall alongside her head and leaned closer. His voice dropped to a captivating purr, flowing over her like a gentle caress. "I was worried about you. I should have known you'd be fine."

Some of his dusty brown hair fell forward, shadowing his eyes, but she didn't need to see his eyes to feel his intent. The awkward moment with Ash on the rooftop danced to the forefront of her mind. She didn't need this confusion right now. She pressed back into the wall, ready to duck away. Maybe she hadn't discouraged him the last time he kissed her, had perhaps even encouraged it a little, but that didn't mean...

He put his other hand to her cheek and she froze, her train of thought careening off its tracks. Her gaze drifted to his lips before it occurred to her that he might take that as permission. He slid his fingers under her chin. The feather light touch sent a shiver through her. She gave in to his gentle pressure, tipping her head back. A wash of anticipation melted away her resistance and perhaps her better judgment. The heat in the room quadrupled when he moved his lean body closer still. His breath warmed her lips. She closed her eyes.

That's about enough of that."

Maeko started and Chaff jerked away, turning toward the speaker. Em stood watching them, her expression anything but charitable. Visions of blackmail danced in Maeko's head when she met the shrewd woman's eyes. If Lucian found out about this, she would be forever confined to the flat at the top of the Airship Tower.

Em stepped one foot forward, hands resting on her hips, pushing back her long coat so that her underarm holster peeked out. "I was under the impression we had an appointment. Imagine how insulted I was when I saw you taking off in that coach. I had to follow and see what was so blasted important. That is what I do, after all."

Maeko felt her cheeks growing hot. She'd been so busy tailing the boy that she hadn't noticed someone else tailing her. Chaff was going to be seriously brassed off.

Em's gaze swept over Chaff. She dismissed him with bitter smirk and focused on Maeko. "I imagine Mr. Folesworth would appreciate my timing."

Chaff turned on Maeko, a different kind of passion flashing in his eyes now.

Prepare for a storm.

"You led *her* here. What's wrong with you?" He made a rough gesture to her skirt. "You get some coin and fancy togs and your wits seep out your ears?"

Oh how she hated it when he was right. Maeko the street rat wouldn't have been that careless. Maybe she could blame it on the corsets, not enough oxygen to the brain or something. She started to draw on that pleading look he could never resist. "Chaff—"

"No. This isn't something you get to sweet talk your way out of." He pointed toward Em and the exit. "Get out."

Sensing the new tension in the air, Macak laid his ears back and sprinted over to leap up on her shoulders. His landing was less graceful this time, striking off a painful spasm in her healing shoulder. She flinched and reached a hand up to adjust his feet.

Em gazed on with a smug smirk and raised her eyebrows at Maeko as if to say, 'I saw this coming.'

Maeko drew in a breath, struggling to fight back the sudden heat of her rising temper.

I'm angry at Em and I'm angry at myself, not him. If I yell at him now, I'll regret it later.

"Now!"

The demand shattered her tenuous composure. Frustration and rage burned high, blazing red at the edges of her vision. Crouching low on her shoulders, Macak hissed at Chaff, his upset adding fuel to the fire. "Fine then. I don't need this ash heap and I certainly don't need any help from you." She turned and started to stalk away.

His soft reply stopped her mid-stride. "You never did."

She spun, nearly throwing the cat off, but Chaff ducked under a fallen timber angled across the hall and vanished around the corner. She stared after him. How strange that it hurt to breathe now, as if someone had driven a dagger into her chest. Her shoulder and arm throbbed, the older injuries there upset by the tussle with the boy and Macak's bad landing, but that was a different and far more tolerable pain, one she welcomed the distraction of now.

First she'd turned Ash away and now she'd let Chaff down. This privileged life was starting to feel very lonely. Lucian would be pleased.

She turned and stormed past Em to lead the way out of the building. The fancy boots and hat she had left inside the entrance were gone, snatched by some opportunistic thief. She should have expected as much. Adding that to the torn dress, the black eye and the bloody lip, she didn't think Lucian was going to be so delighted to see her this evening.

Would Em tell him what she'd seen? Probably not, since it would require the detective admitting that she'd been in contact with Maeko. But if she did...

Lucian had already given her one warning about being alone with boys despite how ridiculous that was. She had spent many a night camped out in lurks like this one where she was the only girl and nothing terrible had come of it, though there had been a near incident or two. Of course, that had all been before Chaff expressed a more intimate interest in her.

How did things get so complicated so quickly? When had he decided that he liked her in that way?

She stopped, resting a hand on one of the rough slats that boarded up the front door. The wood was coarse, the upper boards ragged with splinters and thick with dust. More dust danced in spears of grey light creeping in between the boards from outside. Life on the streets was hard and miserable, but she'd felt more at ease since stepping out of the coach and coming in here than she had yet to feel for even a second in the fancy flat at the top of the Airship Tower. Only she had worn out her welcome here with lighting speed.

She dug her nails into the old soft wood.

Em cleared her throat and Maeko climbed through the slats, adding a few more snags to the damaged dress, then stomped down the street until she saw the familiar coach. She jerked open the door and preceded Em into the shadowed interior, dropping sullenly onto the seat. Unbalanced by her angry motions, Macak leapt down and curled in the far corner, giving her a sullen glower.

Splendid. Now even the cat's brassed off at me.

She examined a tear in the skirt of the dress with feigned interest, swallowing against the tightness in her throat. Em rapped on the roof as she sat across from Maeko and the coach began to move.

"I really can't fathom why you were going to let that street rat kiss you."

"I don't see where it's any business of yours. Besides, it let me get close enough to take this back." Maeko held up her hand and dangled the coin purse.

Em nodded approval. "You are a clever rat. Remind me to keep my valuables in hand when you're around."

Maeko dropped the purse into her lap. A hollow victory. After what had happened, it would only make Chaff that much more upset with her.

"What did you learn about the will?"

"You have to promise me something before I tell you anything."

Em pressed her lips in a tight line and sat back, crossing her arms in a show of stubborn resistance, but Maeko wasn't about to let the woman discourage her. Stubborn was a game they could both play.

"Promise me you won't tell the Lits about that place or you get nothing from me."

Em uncrossed her arms and began to pick absently at the bandage on the side of her neck. "Means that much to you does he?"

Does he?

Maeko said nothing. She waited, staring into Em's

eyes with bleak resolve. Chaff had been mad at her before. That she could live with, though forgiveness wouldn't come easily for this one, if ever, and that left her feeling gutted, but if the Lits raided his primary hideout, he and all of his boys would pay for her carelessness with their freedom at the very least. She would never be able to forgive herself if that happened.

Macak hopped up suddenly and walked over to nudge his head under one hand, curling next to her when she started to pet him. It lifted her mood a fraction and she managed a small smile for the cat.

Thanks, mate.

Em touched the center of the bandage and winced. "All right. I've got a few reasons to suspect that the people behind the shooting the other night might be higher ups in the Literati structure. Since it nearly got me killed and laid Rueben up with a bullet in the arm, I'm in no hurry to do the Lits any favors. They aren't on my list of favorite people right now."

Maeko couldn't stop a sneer. "Is anyone?"

Em glanced at the black ceiling of the coach as if the answer were written there. Her smile was empty, bitter. "No. Not really."

"Why do you hate so much?"

The smile faded. Em exhaled and looked down at Maeko's dirty stockings poking out below the hem of the damaged skirt. "The will?"

"What about the clothes you promised?"

Em shook her head. "I'm already giving you a ride back to the Tower and my word not to tell the Lits about the hideout. You're little excursion is cutting into time that should have been spent on other jobs. I'll need something more in exchange for the clothes."

Fair enough. "The only will I could find everything going to his wife and daughter. It must be the one he wrote while he was hiding in the warehouse, before he knew they were dead. If he has another, I couldn't find it."

Em sat back, her expression becoming lost in the shadowed interior of the coach. "That doesn't help me, but you did what I asked. Did you come across anything else of interest?"

"There were a lot of curious sketches in the bottom of one cabinet. Weapons, I think."

"Just sketches, not actual patent drawings?"

Maeko nodded.

"Fascinating. I'd love to get my hands on those." She chewed at her lip for a moment, her gaze turning inward. "I'll bet a lot of people would," she murmured. Her eyes refocused on Maeko. "I'll drop you around the corner from the Tower. I'd like to meet up again tomorrow. Same time and place, if you think you can be bothered to show up."

The jab had no effect. The weight of Maeko's guilt muted her temper for the moment. "If I can get out of the flat after what happened today."

"That's your problem. I may need you to get in touch with your contacts on the street to help me find someone."

Her hand tightened on the coin purse. She should have let Chaff keep it. "Chaff was my best contact," she snapped.

"Looked to me like he was on board for all kinds of contact. You'd be better off avoiding him if you ask me."

"Did I ask you?"

Em leaned forward, resting her elbows on her knees. Her eyes drilled into Maeko. "I'm sure Mr. Folesworth would be interested in hearing about your relationship with that street rat."

Maeko matched her posture. "Almost as interested as he would be in you dragging me into your investigations. I bet he'd love to know what you're investigating too."

Em sat back again and, to Maeko's surprise, she grinned. Probably the first grin Maeko had ever seen make it into the grouchy detective's eyes. "I don't suppose I'll ever like you much, Rat, but I respect your spirit." The coach rolled to a stop. "I'll have some proper street clothes for you when we meet next time."

That's a relief.

Maeko drew Macak in to her chest and climbed wordlessly out of the coach. The grit-covered pavement was cold and damp under her feet from a recent rain. Several pedestrians gave her bedraggled countenance long startled stares. One woman went so far as to ask if she were okay. Maeko waved her off. She smelled the bakery when she came around the corner of the building. The rich aroma made her stomach growl. Her hand tightened on the coin purse and she stopped to consider. She could still get bread for dinner if they would even serve her in her current state.

A light touch on her hand caught her attention. She looked down into deep brown eyes staring up at her out of a dirt-smudged face. The boy wore tattered, stained clothes and smelled of something from out of a dumpster. She'd smelled that way herself more than once. She wasn't far from it now.

He stared into Macak's eyes as he spoke. "Could ye spare a copper, Miss. Me mum is real sick."

Maeko smiled. The boy had a lot to learn if he were selecting someone in her disheveled condition as his mark. She gathered her skirts and crouched in front of him, letting Macak's feet rest on her thighs. The boy started to reach toward the cat then shied back a step, uncertain. She crooked a finger at him. After a long pause, he inched closer, eyes darting about for any sign of a trap.

"You can pet him."

Wary, he held a finger out. Macak touched his nose

to it and the boy smiled. He inched a bit closer to stroke the cat's head.

"You working for Chaff?" His eyes widened. Confirmation enough. Chaff had been a busy bloke over the last month, branching out into new areas and drawing in new recruits. She took the hand that was petting Macak and put the coin purse in it. "Can you take this to him for me?"

The boy nodded and closed his small fist tight around the purse. Maeko put a hand on his shoulder to keep him from running off and turned to skim the street. It only took a few seconds to find what she wanted. She turned back to the boy and smiled conspiratorially.

"See the woman in the light blue dress leaving the bakery?" He nodded. Not much for talking, this one. Probably for the best. "I bet she'll give you something to line your pockets before you head back."

He glanced at the woman then gave Maeko a dubious look.

"Give it a try." She nodded encouragement.

The boy pocketed the purse and Maeko got up, going to watch from outside the entrance to the Airship Tower. The woman in the blue dress was walking past the boy now. He touched her hand and she stopped, bending down to listen to him. After a brief exchange, she dug into her bag and handed him a few coins, smiling at him sadly before moving on. The boy glanced around, spotted Maeko and grinned. She winked back and stepped on the panel to open the steam-powered doors.

Now to face Lucian.

It took all Maeko's persuasion skills to convince the desk attendant and guards in the lobby that they didn't need to summon an officer, she didn't need medical attention, and it wasn't necessary for someone to assist her up to the tenth floor. What she needed they couldn't provide and that was a way to explain it all to Lucian. There was only one explanation that wouldn't get her into trouble and it wasn't far off the truth, but she was likely to end up with even more restrictions on her freedom no matter how she presented it.

Standing outside the white door to the flat, with its elaborate floral carved frame and shiny brass numbers, Maeko stared down at her dirt-stained stockings and considered going back downstairs and leaving this prosperity rubbish to those more suited to it. Lucian might be upset for a little while, but maybe it would be better in the end. He didn't need her making his life more difficult. It would be hard to leave the certainty of regular meals and warm nights behind. Still, a month wasn't enough time to get used to that kind of thing. She would reacclimatize to her old life fast enough.

A soft head butted against her leg.

Macak.

Her chest ached at the thought of leaving the cat. She took a deep breath and pressed down the thumb lever on the fancy brass handle. The door swung in. She picked Macak up, hoping they hadn't noticed the cat's absence and would think that he had come to the door to greet her. She held his warm body to her chest like armor, then took a deep breath and entered the flat. The unexpected sweet smell of pipe smoke wafted around her. As soon as the door clicked shut, Lucian strode into the front room from the kitchen... twice.

Maeko stared, aware her mouth was hanging open, but unable to fix it as the first Lucian hurried over to grab hold of her shoulders, taking in everything from her bruised eye down to her bare feet with an expression of rising alarm. The other Lucian stayed back, leaning against the doorframe, and shook his head at them before taking a long draw on the pipe in his hand. The two men wore different suits and the one by the kitchen had a haughty scowl under his neatly trimmed moustache, but the differences ended there.

"Good heavens! What happened to you?"

Maeko forced her attention to the concerned Lucian still gripping her shoulders. "Someone nicked my coin purse."

"And then what, you were run over by a hansom?"

The snide comment came from the Lucian in the doorway and concerned Lucian gave him a sharp warning glance. The man by the kitchen shrugged and resumed sucking at his pipe.

"I ran after him. I had to take off the boots. I couldn't run proper in them. I caught him, but he got away from me again and someone nicked the boots while I was gone."

"It looks like the thief had quite the right hook too."

This time concerned Lucian turned fully around to face his double. "Thaddeus, if you don't have anything constructive to contribute then perhaps you could give us a moment alone."

The other Lucian, Thaddeus apparently, shrugged again and tugged a watch out of his pocket to check the time. He didn't leave. Constance peeked around him in the doorway and made a small choking sound before ducking back into the kitchen.

Lucian turned back to Maeko. "Are you hurt?"

"It looks worse than it is," she muttered.

He squeezed her shoulders. "I appreciate your courage, Maeko, but proper young ladies leave the tackling of thieves to men. I had hoped to introduce a lovely young lady to my brother." Thaddeus chuckled, the sound turning to a cough at Lucian's irritated glance. "Go to your room and Miss Foster will help you clean up. Then we can handle proper introductions."

Twins. At least she wasn't hallucinating. "Yes, sir." Maeko lowered her gaze, still clutching the purring cat to her chest, and started down the hall to her borrowed room. She felt Thaddeus watching her, his haughty superiority pressing in on her like a giant vise.

"You'll never take the street out of that one, Lucian. She's worse than the cat."

"Don't be disparaging, Thaddeus. She has a good heart. She just needs opportunity and proper guidance."

Her chest felt heavy when she slipped into the room and set Macak on the bed. Why did Lucian have to defend her? Anger or disappointment she could handle. Although, now that she thought about it, she'd gotten about as much as she could handle of that from Chaff today.

Getting changed and cleaned up required suffering through Constance's ongoing declarations of dismay at the state of her clothes. The maid was almost in tears over the various tears and snags in the fabric. When she was once again properly dressed, she emerged to find Captain Garrett also there and had to suffer his smirk of amusement while Lucian awkwardly explained the black eye and split lip. After proper introductions were made between her and Thaddeus Folesworth, dinner was served, giving her the opportunity to sit and fade silently into the background.

Thaddeus, it turned out, had arrived unannounced to offer support to his brother in his time of loss, though he didn't strike Maeko as the supportive type. More than anything, he appeared to be there to tell Lucian how he should go about his mourning and express his disapproval of Maeko. Garrett, on the other hand, was there to discuss business. He was now working with Lucian on a human variation of Macak's clockwork leg, with the intent of using his disabled younger son as an eventual recipient for the prosthesis. Thaddeus expressed keen interest in the monetary potential of their work.

"You believe you can construct the parts to adapt Lucian's design for human use without adding significant bulk or weight?" Thaddeus leaned on the table, his attention keenly tuned to Garrett's reply.

Garrett's short, spiky hair and the flair of Pirate eccentricity in his attire—brass accented epaulettes on his jacket and leather bracers peeking out under the cuffs—looked markedly out of place at that table, but it didn't appear to bother him. His good-natured smile never faltered. "I don't believe it. I know it."

Thaddeus smiled, polite enough on the surface, though there was a certain sharpening of his interest that struck Maeko as curious. "Could it be adapted it to other things, say a human arm or something along those lines."

"I've heard whispers on the streets that someone has already been experimenting in that area, though I haven't seen anything myself," Garrett started. "Hands are complicated, but now that I understand how the leg works, I'm sure I could figure it out."

Garrett began to go into detail on the technology and science involved and Maeko felt her eyes glazing over. She was happy her efforts had introduced him to Lucian and that both were getting what they wanted out of the arrangement, but she didn't have the education or technical experience needed to keep up with their enthusiastic discussion of complex engineering.

Unexpectedly, Thaddeus was the one who came to her rescue. "I think this is a bit deep for the young lady. Perhaps she would like to go up to the airship landing for some fresh air and take a look at a true marvel of science."

Lucian considered her a moment and managed a slight smile. "Yes, Maeko, you should have a look at the new airship Thaddeus arrived in. It is lovely to behold."

Thaddeus sat back in his chair and crossed his arms. "What he isn't telling you is that it's his airship. I'm only borrowing it. You see, Lucian has all the real money in the family."

Maeko shifted in her seat, unsettled by the searing jealousy in his voice. Lucian didn't seem to notice, or perhaps the scathing tone was so familiar he no longer let it ruffle him. If anyone spoke of her in such a tone, she would sleep with one eye open and keep a knife under her pillow whenever they were around, but maybe that was paranoia born of living on the streets.

"Perhaps Miss Foster would accompany you," Lucian suggested.

Thaddeus waved a dismissive hand at his brother. "Really, Lucian. Must you smother the girl? I'm sure she can handle a stroll to the rooftop without an escort."

Maybe Thaddeus had a few redeeming points after all.

Thaddeus smiled at her then and it wasn't a nice smile. "You'll be safe enough, dear girl. I'm sure there aren't any nasty pickpockets up there."

She smiled back acidic sweetness. "Only this one."

Garrett choked on a laugh, but Lucian didn't look at all amused, nor did his brother.

Thaddeus sneered, his nose wrinkling as if he'd caught wind of a night soil deposit. "Charming."

Lucian stood, giving his twin a stern look. "If you're done giving Maeko a lesson in childish bad manners, Thaddeus, perhaps you would like to join the adults in the sitting room."

Thaddeus lowered his gaze, though he didn't look at all sorry for his conduct.

Lucian met her eyes over the table. "Maeko, you may go up to the dock if you wish, but do take a shawl, there is quite a chill in the air this evening."

"Yes, Sir. Thank you."

In her room, she wrapped an ivory shawl around her shoulders and gazed into the vanity mirror for a moment. The swell around her eye wasn't that bad. There was a small puff around the split in her lip too. She'd had far worse. The boy had been fast enough, but there wasn't much force behind his punches. Chaff needed to teach him some of the moves he'd taught her to help counter the size disadvantage.

Chaff.

She touched a finger to her lip, surprised by a swell of disappointment for that interrupted kiss. Would the coin purse do anything to quell his anger? Would the boy even give it to him?

Macak jumped to the vanity and up onto her shoulders, balancing himself there. She smiled and scratched his head.

"So you think I need a chaperone to go upstairs after all." She left the room, comforted and warmed by the cat's presence. "If only Lucian would let you be my chaperone all the time."

She padded through the kitchen, avoiding the sitting room on her way out. Lucian might not want her taking Macak up to the dock and she'd already dodged one bullet in regards to the cat today. Macak was the only one not upset with her for one reason or another and she needed a little of that kind of company. By the time she stepped out onto the airship dock, her strides relaxed to normal, or as normal as they ever were in heels, and Macak shifted with her movement like an extra appendage.

Captain Garrett's patched up airship loomed like some vast behemoth over a sleek, silvery airship with a comparatively narrow body and a gondola half the size of the other. It looked rather like a fish. She approached the smaller airship cautiously, aware that Macak might not like the airships up close. She wanted to be able to catch him if he started to spook.

Macak, however, stared at the contraption with wide curious eyes, not even startling when she moved under the edge of the main body to peer in a gondola window. The inside gleamed with polished metals of brass, silver, and bronze. The controls, a wide array of levers, switches and gauges were set in a console that wrapped around one large plush chair. An airship designed so that it could be flown by a single person. Several comfortable looking chairs were positioned in the body of the gondola for passengers. The floor had short pile carpeting over it and fancy red and gold brocade curtains were tied back from the windows with braided gold cord.

She heard footsteps approaching. A glance in the window's reflection showed Ash walking up beside her, his hands tucked in his trouser pockets and his broad shoulders hunched. She shifted her gaze back to the interior, focusing on the bright brass Clockwork Enterprises symbol on the control panel.

"Makes ours look like a junk heap, doesn't it?"

"Seems kind of stuffy and presumptuous to me. I'd rather ride in something with a little more character."

She glanced at Ash's reflection in time to catch a glimpse of his fleeting smile.

"Maybe I can talk Dad into taking you up sometime."

"I'd like that." She drew in a breath and faced him.

He avoided her gaze and reached up instead to scratch Macak on the head. The cat pushed into his hand, increasing the pressure on her healing shoulder. She dropped the shoulder a touch and the cat adjusted his stance, moving his feet off the tender scar.

Better.

Ash turned to stare into the gondola. "I'm sorry about last night. I—"

"Please don't apologize."

He finally looked at her, then did a double take. "What happened to you?"

She exhaled and looked away. Macak head-butted her cheek, demanding more attention and she automatically complied, earning an enthusiastic purr. "I got in a tussle with a pickpocket."

"Oh." He managed to look almost concerned for a few seconds, then a smile jerked its way across his lips and he started to laugh. "I can just see you all done up in a nice dress tackling some thief. How surprised must he have been?" He laughed harder yet.

A grin tugged at her lips, but it wasn't enough to lift her mood. "Too bad Mr. Folesworth didn't find it so amusing."

Ash controlled himself and grinned at her. "He'll get used to you."

"Maybe," she replied, wondering if that would ever happen. Probably about the same time she got used to him she supposed. The far side of never perhaps.

"You want to go inside the Mariah?"

Maeko struggled to hold back the laugh bubbling up from her gut. "Mariah? Isn't that a rather dainty name for that bulky thing?"

"Hey, be nice," Ash chastised, winking to show he wasn't serious. "The old girl's sensitive and she's been in a huff ever since we anchored next to this thing." He gave the new airship a sour look as he led her around it.

The Mariah wasn't sleek and shiny. It wasn't carpeted and refined. It was patched and scarred and the inside burst with the smells of grease and bare metal. Garrett's band had etched their logo and their names in the front control panel and various playbills for their performances plastered the walls, set at all angles. Sharp edges abounded, waiting to prod a careless crewman into line.

Two of the Pirate band members sat in mismatched chairs in the gondola smoking and joking. Jack, the younger dark haired chap with his fastidious grooming appeared oddly out of place in the haphazard interior. The other was Warren, a long, skinny older bloke with his mostly bald pate hidden under a tall top hat.

The two men welcomed Maeko into the airship. They teased her about her tussle with the thief when Ash explained her injuries, but the teasing held a glimmer of admiration for her daring that she appreciated. She settled into the airship to chat with them while Macak wandered around, poking his nose into every corner of the gondola. It was comfortable there. They didn't treat her like a proper lady or expect her to behave like one and their presence kept things from getting awkward with Ash again.

Ash commented once on how it was a bit too warm in the gondola and she disagreed, thwarting an obvious attempt to get her alone. She wasn't ready to discuss the two of them. He didn't try again.

Eventually Garrett came out and she made her quick goodbyes, catching a glimpse of frustration in Ash's eyes she hurried off. Constance was waiting in her borrowed room when she got there, ready to help her out of her clothes.

"Where are Lucian and his brother," Maeko asked as she wriggled out of the dress.

"They retired to Mr. Folesworth's study."

Opportunity was passing her by.

Maeko tried not to fidget while Constance helped her out of the rest of her clothes and she donned a nightdress. As soon as the maid turned out the lights and left, Maeko slipped into her robe and crept down to the end of the hall, careful not to make any noise that would alert the two women cleaning up in the kitchen or the men in the study. She crouched down in the shadows and put her ear to the edge of the door, holding one hand out to Macak who trotted down the hall, his leg whirring and clicking, to join her.

"I will not send her away," Lucian snapped. When he continued, it was in a calmer voice. "I'm thinking about making her my legal ward."

Maeko's chest tightened. There was only one 'her' they could be talking about and the idea of being legally bound to Lucian terrified her. This lifestyle was proving to be something she simply didn't have a knack for. What would he expect of her in return for making her his legal ward? Would he expect her to fill the place of his dead daughter in his life?

"That's a fool's fancy, Lucian. She's a creature of the streets. When you've had time to come to terms with your losses, you will realize that. Taking that girl in is a mistake."

"You said that about the cat as well."

Speaking of the cat, Macak forced his way into her lap and curled there, content to nap and purr while she eavesdropped.

"The cat that follows her everywhere? They're kindred beasts. Feral creatures recognize their own kind."

Lucian was silent.

"Besides, if I had known you meant to use that

mangy stray as a test subject for a prototype I might have been more understanding. I don't suppose you have similar plans for the girl. Something that would improve her attitude. A clockwork brain perhaps."

Offensive lout.

"Thaddeus, don't be vulgar. That girl saved my life."

"Yes, and that hasn't worked out in her favor at all."

Maeko bristled at the insinuating tone. How she would love to give the pompous toff a taste of street discipline.

"I doubt she risked her life on the unlikely chance I would take pity on her."

Thaddeus snorted. "You always were the gullible one."

There was a longer silence then and Maeko itched to know what was going on behind those doors. Why didn't Lucian put Thaddeus in his place? Was he starting to doubt her now?

"There may be some truth to that," Lucian blew out a heavy exhale, "but I trust the girl and I do not believe that trust is misplaced."

"Don't come whinging to me when she makes off with all your valuables."

"When are you heading back," Lucian inquired, pushing the conversation in a new direction.

Not soon enough.

"Tomorrow perhaps. Maybe the next day."

From there they moved on to talk of a more political nature and Maeko settled back into the corner to pet Macak while she listened.

There was a creaking of someone settling into a chair.

"Who do you think did it?" Thaddeus asked.

"The commissioner's murder?" Silence in which Thaddeus must have nodded. "I can only guess. The Pirates blame the Literati, citing the rivalry between them and the Bobbies as motivation. The Lits are turning that back on the Pirates, accusing them of committing the crime in order to frame them and raise anti-Literati sentiment. There's no way to know unless they find the one who pulled the trigger."

"It's already led to some good." Thaddeus paused, perhaps to take a pull of his cigar or a drink of whatever liquor they were certainly enjoying. "I hear two Pirates were killed in that shootout over in Southwark this morning."

"And a six year old girl who had nothing at all to do with it," Lucian snapped.

"Every war has its casualties," Thaddeus returned, unruffled. "When did you become so sentimental? You know this conflict needs to be resolved. It will only get worse if the Pirates aren't put in their place."

She could hear someone walking around the room and imagined Lucian pacing, agitated.

"And what place is that?" Lucian asked. "No. Don't answer that. I'm retiring. I've no head for this tonight."

That was her cue to leave. Maeko lifted the ball of fur curled in her lap and slunk back to her room.

s much as she didn't care for Thaddeus Folesworth, Maeko wasn't above using his presence to her advantage. When time for her meeting with Em drew near, she waited for the opportune moment to interrupt the two brothers. They had been sitting in the front room for a few hours. Their conversation, picking up from the previous night, escalated into a heated argument about Pirate activists, Lucian speaking somewhat in their favor and Thaddeus vehemently against them.

She stepped into the room and cleared her throat, only to be ignored by both men. Louder perhaps? By the third try, they finally looked at her, faces reddened by the heat of their anger and perhaps a few too many sips of brandy.

She offered her best polite smile. "Mr. Folesworth," she began, fully aware of the special ambiguity the name carried at that moment, "might I be allowed to go down to the bakery and pick up bread for supper, to make up for yesterday's mishap."

She clung to her smile, ignoring the sour smirk Thaddeus gave her.

Lucian had already begun to shake his head. "I don't think that's a good idea after yesterday. Perhaps Miss Foster could go with you when she and Margaret return."

Maeko had counted on the fact that the two brothers argued over most everything and Thaddeus wasn't going to let her down. He coughed into his hand. Lucian gave him a warning glare that might have kept most people silent. Thaddeus was up to the challenge.

"In all honesty, Lucian, what are the chances of that happening twice in a row? You should let the girl stretch her legs a bit. If you don't give a caged dog some exercise, it's like to become vicious."

It was hard not to react to the cruel comparison, but she sucked back her rage. Em represented an opportunity, one she would likely lose if she failed to show up again. "Please. I'll be careful," she pleaded, keeping her eyes on Lucian to avoid succumbing to the intense urge to glare at his brother.

Lucian still shook his head, not fully convinced, but he stood and dug some coppers out of his pocket for her. She held out the coin purse that matched her pale grey dress and he dropped them in before settling back into his chair.

"Thank you. I won't let you down." She started toward the door, making as if to leave then stopped and turned back as if an idea had only just occurred to her. "Might I be allowed to stop by the coffee house as well?"

Lucian grimaced.

Thaddeus smirked and stood himself, handing her a few more coppers. "My treat, so long as you hurry off and let us continue our conversation in peace."

"Thank you." *May Macak bite your nose off while you sleep.* The thought made it easier to smile at him before hurrying out of the flat. No sense giving Lucian time to reconsider or Thaddeus time to say something that would break the shaky hold she had on her temper in his presence. She knew he was baiting her, but knowing that didn't make it any easier to ignore.

Macak tried to slip out the door with her. She blocked him with her foot and clicked the door shut.

Sorry mate, not this time.

As soon as she stepped outside the lobby into a cold dreary grey that threatened rain, the young boy from the previous afternoon sprang away from the side of the building and trotted over to her. He held a trembling hand out to her. Wary of the desk attendant and guards who might be watching from inside the building, she guided the boy to the corner with a hand on his shoulder then crouched down to face him. He said nothing, only held out his closed hand again. She held her palm out and he dropped something into it.

A set of lock picks. A knot unwound inside her, leaving effervescent giddiness in its place. She grinned. Perhaps she hadn't worn out her welcome with Chaff after all.

The boy stood shifting from foot to foot.

Wants a reward for his trouble no doubt.

Maeko dropped the lock pick set into her coin purse and dug out two pence. The boy snatched the coins from her palm and darted away. Still grinning with her coin purse held firmly in hand this time, Maeko trotted across the busy street to the coffee house.

"What's got you in such a disgustingly sprightly mood," Em asked as soon as Maeko managed to weave through the press of customers to join her at a little table in the back corner.

Despite the crowd, no one had tried to sit in the empty chairs near them. Given Em's frosty glower, Maeko wasn't surprised.

She sat, warming her hands around the coffee she'd bought, and shrugged. "Nothing important." Em didn't need to know about her interactions with Chaff via the young boy, especially given her apparent dislike for him. "Lucian's brother is visiting."

"Thaddeus is here." Em tapped a finger on the table. "That's interesting. Charming bloke, isn't he?"

Em sounded serious and Maeko could think of nothing to say that wouldn't come across as rude, so she held her tongue. Thaddeus had hired Em to find his brother when Lucian went missing so the woman had met him, but she still couldn't help wondering if they were talking about the same man.

Em shifted close, lowering her voice. "Learn anything new?"

Maeko told her about Captain Garrett working with Lucian then recounted the conversation she had heard in the study and what she'd heard of their argument that morning, skipping the part about Lucian's idea of making her his legal ward. Em would probably support Thaddeus in that dispute and Maeko wasn't sure yet which side she was on.

The detective listened in tight lipped silence then shook her head. "There isn't much I can use there. Though partnering with a Pirate activist on a project of this importance is worth noting as is his relative support of the Pirates in their cause."

"You know what I found interesting?"

"No, but I'm sure you'll tell me," Em remarked.

"Maybe I won't."

Em gave her a hard look.

Maeko relished the detective's irritation for a moment, taking several slow sips from her drink before speaking again. "Not once when they were talking about the commissioner's murder did Lucian mention that he'd met with the man the night he was killed."

Em stared at her for several seconds then her head bobbed in a slow nod. "You're right. That is interesting. Whatever he was up to with the commissioner, he doesn't even trust his own brother enough to speak of it. I would have thought they had a closer relationship considering the effort Thaddeus put into finding him when he went missing. How long is he visiting for?"

"He's supposed to be leaving tonight or tomorrow."

Em sighed. "Too bad. I'd like to learn a little more about that relationship." She reached under the table and brought up a brown satchel. She shifted a little closer still and set it on the floor between them, then leaned over and spoke in a whisper. "The clothes I promised are in here. I need you to ask around on the streets. I believe the men who killed the commissioner were hired thugs. One of them had—"

"You were there?"

Em scowled at her interruption.

"Sorry."

"Yes. That's how I got the wound on my neck. It's a long story and it doesn't matter right now. I didn't get a good enough look at the individual I believe shot the commissioner, but there was another shooter on the rooftop. He was a big bludger with a limp, a hip injury from the way he moved, and he appeared to have what could have been a cast on his right forearm. He wore a long tattered coat and a wide-brim slouch hat. See if that description catches anyone's attention. Don't tell them why you're looking. You might warn them not to go near him though. He may have a limp, but he can move fast enough."

Her mouth had gone a bit dry, so she took another sip of her drink.

Ask around about an accomplice in a high profile murder. Nothing dangerous or potentially incriminating. "Is that all?"

"For now. I have another case to wrap up. I'll meet you again in three days." Without any ceremony, Em snapped to her feet and strode from the establishment.

Maeko stayed for a short time longer, sipping at her coffee and pondering ways to get the satchel into the flat without drawing attention. When she had an idea, she walked to the bakery for bread and returned to the Airship Tower. The attendant on duty was a young man with a goofy smile and big ears. He flushed every time she spoke to him, which she'd decided to take as a compliment of sorts. Today was no exception, his pale complexion brightened to pink before she even reached the desk.

"How can I help you, Miss?"

His voice cracked on the 'miss' and she had to swallow a giggle. She set the satchel on the desk. "Could you be a dear and hold onto this for me for a few hours?"

"Of course, Miss." He took the satchel and tucked it behind the counter. "Just let me know when you need it. It'll be safe and sound till then."

"Thank you. You're very sweet."

She turned to walk away when an explosion split the air. The sound jolted through her, setting her nerves on fire. She dropped the bread on the desk and sprinted to the front doors, stopping shy of running outside. Burning debris rained down alongside the building, falling into a street full of panicked pedestrians and horses. One pair of horses wheeled around so fast they overturned their carriage onto a man running to get away from the plummeting wreckage. His cries added to the chaos. Maeko stared on, frozen in horror as another bolting horse left his discarded rider in lying in the street and collided with a woman running to safety. The woman flew through the air like a ragdoll and hit the ground several feet away. She didn't move again. Burning material caught on the fleeing animal's saddle and stuck there, flame billowing behind as it fled down the street and more people leapt out of its path. Chunks of metal fell into the fray, injuring more startled pedestrians.

In seconds, the street was clear of all but the injured and the hail of burning rubble lessened to a few floating bits of fabric. Maeko stepped out of the building and looked around at the destruction. One large metal section had busted though the window of the coffee house she'd been sitting in minutes ago. People were heading back into the street now to help the injured, glancing up at the sky with nervous expectation. The guards from the Tower moved past her. A section of fabric, burning at the edges, floated down beside her. Red and gold brocade.

Lucian's airship.

Maeko's gaze moved up the Tower to the rooftop landing. Two men stood at the rail staring down. One looked familiar. She sprinted back into the building, pulled off her shoes at the foot of the stairs so she could move faster and hurried up. At the top, she had to stop a few seconds to catch her breath, but it had still been faster than the lift would have been. Dashing through the flat, she burst out onto the airship dock and sprinted for the railing. One figure still stood there. The dock watchman was walking the rooftop, nudging debris around with his foot as if searching for something.

Maeko walked up next to the lone figure by the rail. He gripped the railing tight enough that his knuckles were white and tears streamed unchecked down his cheeks, gathering in his moustache while he stared down at the wreckage below.

"Lucian?" She touched his hand and he jerked it away.

"Leave me." His voice trembled, tight with emotion.

She hesitated, trying to think of something to say, but what did you say to a man who had lost so many loved ones in such a short time. Wrapping her arms around herself against a sudden chill, she turned and trudged back down into the flat. Constance burst through the front door a few seconds after Maeko entered. She held the bread Maeko had forgotten at the front desk in one hand. Her eyes were wide and moist as they swept the room.

"What happened?"

Maeko walked up behind the settee and gripped the back. Macak appeared from somewhere in the rear of the flat and leapt up to place himself in his new favorite spot on her shoulders. She scratched his head absently, soothed by his soft purr, his face pressing warm against her cheek.

"The airship exploded."

Constance's hand went to her chest. "Oh dear God! Thaddeus?"

Maeko shook her head. No one could have survived that.

"Margaret's outside helping with injured folks. Where's Mr. Folesworth?"

"He's up on the dock. He wanted to be left alone."

"And you left him! Good Heavens! We'll be lucky if he doesn't come plummeting down next."

Constance sprinted for the door to the dock, tossing the bread on the dining table on her way past. Maeko scowled after her. Lucian wouldn't jump. She'd heard the anger in his voice. Right now, he felt betrayed. He was furious with the world and that rage would keep despair at bay for a time. Constance could find that out the hard way if she wished.

She stood for a minute, staring around at the fancy flat with its decorative lamps and the many patent drawings hanging in frames on the walls. Wealth didn't do a thing to protect one from tragedy, it seemed. No matter how rich a person was, fate could do as it pleased with them. Knowing that didn't make her feel any better. Would it be different if she were still on the streets? Would seeing a wealthy man suffer this way make her feel like there was justice in the world?

No. It wouldn't, but she probably wouldn't feel so helpless. She wouldn't have this vast hollow in her chest. Thaddeus hadn't been her kin, nor had she liked him all that much, but she wouldn't have wished this on him and she worried what another loss would do to Lucian.

Perhaps she should go downstairs and try to help the injured, though she imagined it was confusing enough already without one more body bustling about. The Lits would be there soon, if they weren't already, and she wasn't keen to get involved with them, even if she did have Lucian's protection now. The attendant still had the clothes Em had given her. He would certainly understand if she chose to retrieve them later when things settled down a bit.

"Come on, Macak, let's go to our room."

She turned to walk around the settee and froze. The side table stood askew of its usual spot, as if someone had bumped it, and the stack of science journals had fallen to the floor. She could imagine Lucian ready to settle in after his brother's departure. Startled by the explosion, he might have bumped the table and knocked the journals off in his rush to go see what had happened. It wouldn't be much, but cleaning up that little mess, that reminder of the tragic moment, might help in some way.

She shifted the table back into place then crouched down, careful not to upset her passenger, and began to pick up the journals, placing them back in a neat stack on the table. When she started to set the last one on top of the stack, something caught her eye. There was a light spatter of red spread across the cover. She examined the red spots and her stomach did a flip, unease building to a wild flutter in her gut.

The sound of someone opening the door from the dock made her start. Clutching the journal, she retreated to her bedroom and sat on the bed, staring at it in the light of the gas sconces. A fine spray swept out across the front cover in the deep rust color of dried blood. Had that been there before? She'd never spent much time studying the journals—they were well above her reading level—but something that out of place should have caught her attention.

She shivered. Macak jumped down from her shoulders and pushed his fuzzy head under her arm.

"I know. I'm worried too, mate." She drew him onto her lap with one hand, still staring at the journal.

What did it mean? Did it mean anything at all? Was she being a paranoid street rat again?

When supper was ready, the maids summoned Maeko from her room and Constance went up, making what Margaret said was her third attempt to coax Lucian down from the rooftop dock. This time he came trudging listless through the door, his suit soaked through with the rain that had started an hour ago. Constance followed behind, twisting her apron in her hands and using it to wipe the occasional tear from her cheeks. Lucian retreated to his study without a word and shut the door. Margaret insisted that Maeko stay and eat something, so she picked at her food, sharing choice bits that she had little appetite for with Macak who curled discreetly on the chair next to her.

When the Literati came to speak with Lucian later in the evening, she snuck around to the hallway and crouched in the shadows to listen. A dark mood thickened the atmosphere in the flat. The sorrow in the air was thick enough to suffocate them all.

"Mr. Folesworth, we found your brother's remains in the wreckage. I'm sorry to say there isn't much left to identify. The coroner will handle that part of things as delicately as possible. However..."

The officer trailed off and his companion spoke into

the awkward silence, a voice she knew and despised.
Officer Tagmet. Their brief encounter the other day
showed that her new status hadn't changed her in his
regard and validated her decision to stay out of sight.

"I am afraid this was no accident," Tagmet declared
indelicately.

"You think someone murdered my brother. Why?
What would they stand to gain from my brother's
death?" Lucian questioned. His voice sounded hoarse,
perhaps from crying.

"The airship belonged to you, correct?"

Silence.

"We suspect they may have been hoping to get
to you. Whoever did it would have had to have access
to the airship since it anchored here. The investigator
said the explosives were set to go off when the engines
engaged. We'll be questioning all the staff and residents
here, servants included. We're asking people not to allow
servants to leave. We need the names of anyone who's
had access to that dock since the airship landed there."

"Garrett Harris docked here last night for a supper
with my brother and I. He and his crew all spent time
up there." There was a brief silence and Maeko held her
breath, knowing who else was about to come up on
the list. "And that girl was up there for some time last
night."

That girl? The phrase was a knife to the gut. When
had she become *that girl?* Did he think she was somehow
involved in all of this? What happened to the trust he'd
spoken of the night before?

"What girl?" Tagmet prompted.

"Ah, yes," Lucian muttered as though recalling
something he'd forgotten. "Maeko."

"The street rat," Tagmet clarified, his tone sharp
with undisguised contempt.

"Yes."

Yes? He'd lost his brother and she was demoted back to street rat status? Maybe it could all be chalked up to his need to lash out at someone for his pain. Maybe she was simply the closest and easiest target, but something didn't feel right. The butterflies in her stomach had grown to the size of ravens.

"Is she here?"

"She's in her room," Lucian answered, his tone picking up some of Tagmet's contempt.

"Good. Keep her and your servants here until we can get to questioning them. Unfortunately, shorthanded as we are, it may take most of the night to get things sorted downstairs. We won't get to questioning people until sometime tomorrow. No one is to leave the building until they've spoken with an investigator. I know this is a hard time for you, but I'm afraid we'll have to ask you respect those terms as well."

"Yes," Lucian answered, sounding impatient now. "Of course."

"Thank you for your time, Mr. Folesworth." The other officer sounded apologetic, trying to smooth over Tagmet's gruff manner.

Maeko slunk back to her room, heart pounding in her ears. Her eyes tracked to the blood-spattered science journal sitting on the bed. Something felt very wrong. Lucian wasn't acting like himself. Was it reasonable to expect him to though, after all the loss he had suffered?

Macak sat beside the journal, watching her with that all-knowing expression that came so naturally to cats. He got up and nudged the edge of the journal with his nose, pushing it toward her. Footsteps approached down the hall. She grabbed the journal and shoved it under the bed. There was a light knock on the door before it swung in without awaiting a response. She looked up at him and he looked back at her, his face a severe, emotionless mask. Macak trotted to the far corner of the bed and jumped off, vanishing underneath. The cat's uncharacteristic behavior made her feel sick.

"You should be in bed."

"Yes, Sir. I just need to get Constance to help me with the dress."

He gave a curt nod. "Get to it then." Without another word, he shut the door and she heard the door to the study close a few seconds later.

He didn't say goodnight. He really wasn't behaving like himself at all. Then again, he had just lost his brother. Maybe she was reading too much into what had to be an overwhelming load of grief. One more loss piled on top of the loss of his wife and daughter. But she had watched him grieve before, when he learned of their deaths. He had welcomed her then, taking solace in her presence even though she was a stranger to him. This time he knew her, had taken her into his home like family. Shouldn't he be more willing to accept her into his grieving process? Unless...

Macak emerged and hopped on her lap. She scratched the sides of his neck and he ducked his head against her chest, closing his eyes and purring.

"You noticed it too, didn't you?" The cat responded with a soft squeak into her clothes. For once in her life, she desperately wanted to be wrong. "What do I do now?"

That was obvious, now that she thought about it. She had to find a way to warn Ash what had happened before the Lits came to question them. If she slipped out now, she could probably sneak out amidst the confusion downstairs. No one downstairs would expect her to make an escape. They all made the same mistake of expecting someone dressed like a young lady to behave like one. She fastened her dress boots on again and stood. Macak leapt to her shoulders and nuzzled her cheek.

"You can't come." The cat nipped her ear hard enough to sting and she caught his head in her hand. "That wasn't nice." Of course, neither was leaving him here if what she feared were true.

Cold swept through her with the startling realization that she didn't intend to return after she warned Ash and his family. If her gut feeling was accurate, trouble was brewing and it didn't bode well for her future. Someone needed to take the fall for Mr. Folesworth's death and it didn't seem likely that it would be the one responsible. Blaming her would get her out of the way, but no one would believe she had pulled such a thing off all by herself. Ash and his family were the next most logical suspects, especially given her association with them in the chaos around the murder of Lucian's wife and daughter.

And if I'm wrong?

Running away might break Lucian's heart yet again if she were wrong. If she were right, however, she stood to lose everything. Even if that man really was Lucian, the loss of his brother had changed something in him. She wasn't willing to gamble her life on it changing back before something bad happened to her or to someone she cared about.

She left the room, opening and shutting the door with the silence of a mouse. She took only the clothes she wore, a matching shawl, a coin purse with the lock pick set Chaff sent her and her key to the flat in it, and the cat on her shoulders. Hushed voices in the kitchen warned her where Constance and Margaret were. They were engaged in tearful conversation about the loss of Lucian's brother and all the sorrow that had struck that household in the last few months, so would be unlikely to notice her if she was careful.

She snuck into the spare room. Thaddeus had spent the night there, though all trace of him had already been cleaned away by the servants. In one corner of the room, tucked behind a blue and silver brocade chair, sat Macak's carrying case. She drew it out and Macak hopped down from her shoulders to climb inside. She nodded gratitude to the cat for his cooperation before closing the case. At least he didn't cause trouble. Perhaps he sensed the gravity of their situation.

Carrying the case with her now, she crept into the front sitting room and dug all the extra money out of the box on the table, tucking it into the coin purse. She heard one of the women in the kitchen moving toward the doorway and ducked behind the settee, recalling the time she had been caught in that position by Em, the night she found Lucian's family dead. That time, she'd given Macak a little squeeze to make him alert Detective Emeraude to her presence. She'd gotten her first taste of what it felt like to stare down the barrel of a gun that night, though it hadn't been her last. She held her breath and hoped for the best. This time, getting caught would serve no purpose. The cat remained silent while Constance put out the light near the door and continued into the dining room to put out those lights as well.

When Constance returned to the kitchen, Maeko tiptoed to the door under the cover of darkness and let herself out, appreciating the silence of the quality hinges and latch now more than ever. By the time she reached the third floor landing, she could hear noise from below, many voices talking over the occasional moan or cry. It sounded as if the lobby had been converted to a base of operations for cleanup and care of the injured. At the ground level, she hung back in the shadows to wait for the right moment. When no one appeared to be looking her way, she slipped out and tucked the case alongside the staircase behind a big planter, laying her shawl over it to hide the holes.

The only one in the crowd below who might cause her a problem was Tagmet, and he'd only once seen her cleaned up and dressed like a girl. He might not notice her if she didn't do anything to draw attention. For the moment, he was standing in the front door bellowing at someone working in the street.

Perfect.

She strode across to the desk as if her heart weren't stuck in her throat and her knees trembling like the pages of windblown leaflets under her skirts. The desk attendant from earlier spotted her coming and nodded, reaching down to pull up the satchel. This time, he started the encounter so pale that his flush made him look a shade better than dead.

"I suppose you want this, Miss?"

"Thank you." She rested her elbows on the desk, fearful that her trembling legs wouldn't hold her upright without the extra support. "I need to run and get something from the apothecary for Mr. Folesworth. Is there another exit so I don't have to go through this chaos?"

He swallowed, his eyes darting around the room. They came to rest on Tagmet for several seconds then sank to his own hands fidgeting on the desktop. "No one's supposed to leave the building, Miss. Officer Tagmet's orders. I'm sorry."

Maeko reached out and took his hands, giving them a gentle squeeze. He swallowed harder and a bright flush accented his high cheekbones. "I'd only be gone a moment. After all Mr. Folesworth has been through today, I couldn't bear to let him down."

The boy's eyes darted to Tagmet again who still stood in the doorway, letting in the cold and holding a shouting match with another officer outside. The young attendant turned back to her and leaned close. She mirrored the motion, leaning in so that their faces were uncomfortably close. Whatever it took to get what she needed. He swallowed again.

"There's an exit at the back of the east conference room. There shouldn't be anyone in there right now. If you flip the little switch on the latch it won't lock behind you, but be sure to lock it on your way back in."

She squeezed his hands again, batting her eyes as she'd seen other women do to unsettle men, though she didn't quite get how it worked. "Thank you so much. I won't forget this."

He nodded, avoiding her eyes. His cheeks blazed like beacons now.

She grabbed the satchel and strode to the stairway to collect Macak's case. With that same confident air, she walked around to the indicated conference room door, snatching up an umbrella someone had left leaning against the wall on her way past, and stepped through the door when no one was looking.

The big room beyond was dark. With the massive lobby and ballroom available, they hadn't needed to use this space. The only risk now was that someone might be watching the door from outside, but being shorthanded meant they weren't likely to have enough men to monitor all the exits. Still, she tiptoed to the waiting door, pausing every few steps to listen. At the door, she pushed down the handle and jumped at the loud click it made. Her heart raced as she inched the door open and peeked out.

No one.

Opening the umbrella to ward off the drizzle, she stepped out and let the door fall shut behind her. She'd almost made it to the corner when a Literati officer stepped around the building and turned her direction.

The officer gave her a puzzled look and held up a hand for her to stop. "Excuse me, Miss."

She stopped in her tracks and let him close the

remaining distance. *Steady, Mae.* "Yes, Officer?"

He frowned, water dripping from his hat added weight to the dour expression. "It's a bit late for a stroll. I'm afraid I'll have to ask you where you appeared from."

"Appeared," she managed a lighthearted titter. "I walked here from a block up. I was taking a hansom from Covent Garden, but there seems to be some incident on Oxford. We've been stuck for a while. I thought it might be faster if I finished the trip on foot. What happened?"

"An airship accident, Miss. Nothing to concern yourself with."

"Oh my." She drew in a sharp breath. Macak shifted around in the case and her muscles strained to keep it still, her arm aching in protest.

The officer placed a hand on his club and tapped his fingers on the handle. A not-so-subtle threat. "As I said, it's a bit late for a young lady like you to be out, especially alone, Miss. Where's your chaperone?"

There it was again, society and its obsession with propriety trying to back her into a corner. "To be honest, Sir, I'd gone alone for a ride in our coach. Father doesn't mind that sort of thing as long as I don't get out and I usually don't. The driver told me to wait until things cleared out, but I got so dreadfully bored. It's just a few more blocks after all."

The officer shook his head, disapproval of her unconventional behavior overpowering his suspicion. "It's your hide, Miss. Best be on your way then. I'd escort you myself, but I can't leave my patrol."

"Thank you, Officer. Have a pleasant evening."

He gave a cynical snort at that, though he did tip his hat when she smiled. Now if she could just get out of sight before her dancing nerves made her heave.

As much as Maeko disliked wearing dresses, once she was away from the Airship Tower, the respectable attire did make it easier to talk a hansom driver into picking her up on his way back to the cabstands. She didn't get any dubious glances or requests to see proof of payment before he accepted the fare. Just a quick smile and a 'Where too, Miss?' as he held the door open for her. Another unexpected benefit of wealthy living that she would miss along with having someone else to make excuses for her. Neither was worth the hassle of trying to be a proper young lady or the danger that she faced if Lucian was no longer himself.

She had the driver drop her a few blocks past Ash's house. It gave her a chance to scan the area for trouble before making her approach. Based on what the Lits said to Mr. Folesworth, they wouldn't get to questioning Ash's family before the next day at the earliest, but one couldn't be too careful, not when another murder accusation was flying around looking for someone to land on.

The house was dark and quiet, its occupants asleep she hoped. It would be easier to talk to Ash than to his parents, who might be less inclined to believe her story. How sure was she that they were all going to land on the chopping block? Sure enough to sneak out of the Tower with Mr. Folesworth's cat in hand. That didn't mean she

couldn't be wrong, which made it even more important
to see a friendly face, someone who might at least listen
to her wild tale before coming to their own conclusions.

With the satchel over one shoulder and Macak's case
dragging down the other arm, she started toward the
house, the black gentleman's umbrella she had nicked
warding off the rain. At their door, she stood for a long
moment, pondering knocking. They all needed to know
what they faced. She wasn't that comfortable around the
rest of Ash's family though. They had been kind enough
to her, but Captain Garrett treated her like a child and
she needed someone to take her seriously right now.

Macak's plaintive meow told her he was growing
weary of his cramped quarters. She tried the door.
Locked. She dug out the lock pick set and made short
work of the simple lock. After listening with her ear
to the door for a silent count to sixty, she crept into
the dark house. Setting her things by the couch, she
removed the boots and padded back to the room she
knew Ash and Sam shared.

The bedroom door stood open a finger's width.
A soft snore sounded through the crack. The hinges
squeaked when she pushed it and she cringed, waiting a
moment to see if either of the boys stirred. Ash rolled,
putting his back to the door, but didn't wake. Samuel,
his false leg on the floor by his bed, muttered something
in his sleep. They weren't street rats. The threat of a
midnight Literati raid or of being robbed because you
had to hole up in an unfamiliar place didn't hang over
their heads, forcing them to sleep light.

That's the life I'm going back to.

She stood there, her hand on the knob, watching
them sleep for a few seconds more.

What if I'm wrong?

The chill down her spine spurred her on. She crept
in and leaned over Ash, touching his shoulder. His eyes

opened and snapped wide when he saw her. She put a finger to her lips then pointed toward the door. He nodded.

Assuming he might not be decent, she left the room and returned to the front. Macak made a small, desperate sound from within the crate. He probably needed out. She picked up the crate and satchel and carried them to the back door, passing Ash's room as he was stepping out. He followed her out the back door and eased it shut behind them.

"What are you doing here," he whispered.

"Something's happened. Wait a second." She bent down and unfastened the crate. The moment it was open, Macak sprinted out and began investigating the small yard.

Ash's mouth dropped open. He shook his head at her. "You've run off with Mr. Folesworth's cat? Have you gone mad?"

"I don't think he'll be missing him." She couldn't speak for a moment, caught off guard by a twist of sorrow that tightened her throat. She and Lucian may have had their differences, but he'd taken her in and tried to make her life better. It was hard to see that opportunity destroyed, to know the man who had tried to give it to her was gone.

Macak found a spot he deemed satisfactory and began to dig a small hole.

"Maeko, what's going on?"

She took a deep breath of cool night air, letting it sooth the ache in her throat, and blinked back the moisture in her eyes. "Thaddeus's airship exploded when it was leaving the Tower today." She held up a hand to stop whatever he was about to say. She needed to get through this fast and get on her way. "The Lits said someone rigged it to blow up when the engines engaged."

His eyes widened. "Murder?"

"Yes. Everyone who's been in the building since the airship anchored there is suspect," she stared hard into his eyes, "especially those of us who were up at the airship dock."

Understanding rose in his eyes and his face blanched, giving him a ghostly look in the pale moonlight. She could imagine all the trials his family had gone through when they were suspects in the death of Lucian's wife and daughter were rushing through his mind. Her heart went out to him. That bollocks had only just gotten resolved. They'd barely had time to get back to normal life.

"But, we haven't done anything wrong. Dad and Mr. Folesworth are working together now. I'm sure he'll clear this up."

She chewed at her lip and turned away, watching Macak pounce on something in the grass. What she wouldn't give to trade places with the cat right now. "That's the problem. I don't think the right Mr. Folesworth was on the airship when it happened."

"I don't understand." The rising edge in his voice told her he understood more than he wanted to admit.

She met his eyes again, making sure she had his full attention. "I think Lucian was on the airship. I think his twin brother Thaddeus is trying to take his place. The Mr. Folesworth in that flat now isn't the same man I found hiding in the warehouse."

Ash shifted back from her, stubborn resistance turning his expression cold.

Anger started to simmer in her gut. How could he not believe her after all they had been through before?

But it wasn't that simple.

"I know they're twins and Dad said Thaddeus was a disagreeable bloke, but I can't believe he's so awful he would kill his own brother. You've only been there about a month. You can't know how Mr. Folesworth would react to his brother's death. I'm sure you're just reading things into his behavior."

"No, I'm not," she hissed. "You weren't there. He wasn't acting like himself at all. And you didn't see how jealous Thaddeus was of Lucian's success. You didn't see how much he disliked me. The man in that flat is not Lucian Folesworth. Even Macak was afraid of him."

His expression remained closed, resistant.

He didn't want to believe her. She couldn't blame him. She didn't want to either. Lucian had been kind to her and it hurt more than she cared to admit to think of him dead, but she felt in her heart that it was true. The certainty made her stomach do flips, but feelings in her heart and gut weren't going to convince Ash.

"After the airship exploded, I found signs of a struggle in the flat and there was blood on one of the science journals. I think they had a fight. Thaddeus could have forced Lucian to leave in the airship or perhaps put him in it and sent it off somehow. You have to believe me. If I'm right, your family is in serious danger."

"I don't know, Mae. I just—"

"Please. All I ask is that you tell Captain Garrett what I told you. At least he'll have some warning and can make an informed decision on how to handle the situation. Please." She pleaded with her eyes and felt a small burst of victory inside when his shoulders sank and the resistance in his eyes broke.

He nodded. "All right. I'll tell him what you said, but, if this is all true, you can't mean to go back there. Where are you going to go?"

"Back where I belong." Why did that answer leave a bitter taste in her mouth? Was it because she didn't want to go back? Had she already become so accustomed to luxury or was it because it took Lucian's death to make her accept that she didn't belong in his world?

Ash stared at her feet, resentment darkening his features. "Back to Chaff?"

"Blast it, Ash, don't do this right now. I'm going back to the streets. Chaff is brassed off at me right now anyway." Maybe not as upset as all that, but Ash didn't need details.

"He is, is he?"

"Yes. Now help me out of this dress. If I go wandering the alleys around Cheapside at night dressed like this Thaddeus Folesworth will be the least of my worries."

He stared at her, mouth hanging open. After a few seconds, he said, "You want me to do what?"

She rolled her eyes at the flush rising in his cheeks, aware that a similar flush now crept into hers. "I can get out of these clothes without help if I have to, but it'll take a lot longer." With that, she put her back to him so he could undo the laces and she could hide her embarrassment. "Now would be great," she said when nothing happened. "Please."

Ash was quiet. Almost a minute passed before she felt his fingers fumbling at the bow and the laces loosened. When it was loose enough, she directed him to help pull it up and off. He handed the dress around in front of her then she pulled off the camisole and set him to work on the corset laces. His fingers trembled so much they tickled her even through the corset. It was all she could do to stand still. Maybe she should have tried to do it alone, though it really would take a lot longer and probably look like a squid trying to escape a fisherman's net.

The flush rose hot in her cheeks now, despite the fact that the extensive ladies undergarments still covered most of her skin. His fingers brushed the back of her neck and the skin tingled in their wake.

"Is that good?" he murmured.

She nodded and made a small noise of affirmation. Odd that she should feel so much more lightheaded now that the corset was loose. "I can get the rest," she said. "Turn around."

Rather than turn his back to her as directed, he took a step closer and the warmth of his body chased away some of the cold that nipped at her skin. His hands came to rest on her shoulders. Warm breath touched the back of her neck.

"Maeko."

She froze with the dress clutched to her chest. How nice would it be to shift back into his arms and let him hold her, let him warm her and drive away the ache of sorrow inside, if only for a moment. If she did that though, she knew it wouldn't stop there. Nor would Chaff consent to stay out of her thoughts now that they strayed towards intimacy with someone else. The confusion already starting to nag at her would only undermine her resistance to the hollow sadness spreading through her chest, a black pit that could swallow her down given half a chance.

Ash pressed closer still and wrapped his arms around her, drawing her back against him. His breath brushed over her skin and it did feel good, and it did make the hurt inside grow. She squeezed her eyes shut against the fresh sting of tears and swallowed, fighting against the urge to lean into him and let him support her.

"Please Ash, I can't. Not right now."

She could feel his heart beat against her back, fast and hard. He didn't let go for several seconds, then he backed away and the cold rushed in, raising gooseflesh on her exposed skin.

"It's not so bad to let someone else in." There was pain and the tightness of unfulfilled longing in his voice. "When will you learn that you don't always have to be the strong one?"

Guilt twisted in her chest. *I should have stopped him sooner.* "When it's true," she whispered.

CHAPTER TWELVE

Ash was silent. When Maeko glanced over her shoulder, he had his back to her, his posture stiff. She folded the dress and set it on Macak's carrier, then swapped out the rest of her clothing as fast as she could manage. The clothes Em had gotten for her fit well. Better, by far, than many of the ragtag clothes she wore during her years on the street. The woman had a good eye for size and had been thoughtful enough to include a wool jacket along with the trousers and shirt. Not only that, but she'd tucked some nice boys shoes and a newsboy hat in the package.

By the time, Maeko had everything on and the dress clothes tucked away in the satchel, her heartbeat had returned to normal, the guilt faded to a distant nagging. She could only hope the time had cooled Ash down as well.

"All done."

Ash turned around and looked her over. A subdued smile tugged at his lips. "You look adorable."

She heaved a sigh. "Adorable wasn't really the look I was going for."

He shrugged. "Sorry. You can't help it."

She almost cried out when something landed on her shoulders, then Macak butted his head against her cheek and she sagged with relief.

Ash did grin then. "See, he agrees with me. What are you going to do with him?"

"I don't know. I'll figure something out." She scratched Macak's chin then kissed him between the ears when he went to push his head into her cheek again.

"I see where I rate. Even the cat gets kisses."

She stuck out her tongue at Ash, figuring from the hint of playfulness in his tone that she could get away with it without offending him. He rolled his eyes and shook his head at her. The fondness in his gaze left a flutter in her chest and she looked away, sinking down to tuck Macak back into his carrier. Ash crouched down to help her. She closed the panel and their hands went to latch the buckle that held the door shut, his landing on top of hers. She hesitated and he closed his hand around hers, sliding his fingers into her palm.

"How can I get in touch with you?"

Why did bleeding boys have to make things so complicated?

She tried to think of an answer that would appease him. There wasn't one. "I don't know."

His hand tightened on hers. He brushed the fingers of his other hand over her cheek, tucking a strand of hair behind her ear. "That isn't good enough. I need to know that you're all right."

She closed her eyes. Would it be this complicated when she saw Chaff again? If so, maybe she shouldn't go there. There had to be somewhere else.

I have to go there. I have to know Em kept her word and...

And she needed to know that Chaff wasn't still angry with her. She drew her hand away from Ash's and latched the case, then stood. He stood with her, somehow ending up much closer than before.

"I'll find a way to get in touch." She made herself meet his eyes, those lovely pale eyes. *Trust me.* The words became stuck in her throat. She swallowed.

Ash stepped even closer, taking her shoulders in his hands. His warm lips touched hers in a light kiss. He drew back too fast for her to protest or respond in kind, or even consider which of those options she wanted to take.

"I can't stand the thought of not seeing you again. I care about you, Mae."

The need in his tone helped her find her voice. "Then trust me." She met his searching gaze steadily and he finally nodded. "I'll be in touch as soon as I can. I promise. Just be careful."

"You be careful too."

She backed out of his hands. Grabbing her things, she hurried through the house, snatching up her dress boots on the way back out into the cold, drizzly night. Eventually, she needed to figure this whole boy bollocks out or she would go barmy with it. Still, it would have to wait for a time. First, she needed to get somewhere she could hide out for a bit and gather her thoughts. Ash was in charge of his own family's safety now. She'd warned him. There wasn't much else she could do.

•

Getting to Cheapside proved easy enough. She ended up sharing a hansom with a gentleman far too inebriated to notice anything amiss about the young *boy* next to him. When Macak meowed, she'd feared there would be trouble, but the man just pointed at the case and burst into hysterical laughter. His top hat fell off and bounced into the street. He didn't notice and she didn't point it out. She had the driver pull off several blocks early to escape the irritating chap's drunken humor, which wasn't nearly as amusing as he thought it was, and walked a circuitous route to the hideout, handing off the umbrella along the way to a woman and two young children huddled alongside an ashbin.

A trio of men watched her pass while they puffed at their cigarettes, but the coat hid her shape and she kept her face averted. They soon lost interest, not willing to leave the shelter of the overhang they stood under. The rain soaked coat began to drag on her shoulders and Macak made an irritated sound to protest the damp creeping into his crate.

She tapped the top of the crate with a finger. "Hush, mate. We're almost there." He only needed to be quiet a little longer.

She came around the side of the boarded up building and started to turn toward the entrance on that side when a sound caught her attention, a mournful desperate whine cutting through the patter of the rain. She stopped and listened. The whine came again. It sounded like a scared or injured dog. She didn't need to be taking in any more animals, but she couldn't just ignore it. It was coming from the alley around the corner.

She crept to the edge and peered around. A large figure cloaked in a tattered blanket hunched over a dog lying on its side in a puddle. The animal was panting hard, its eyes closed, and every other labored breath came forth with that heart-wrenching whine.

Was the person trying to help the dog? Perhaps she should leave him to it. The whine came again, a twisting dagger in her chest.

She entered the alley and took a few steps toward the figure. "Can I help you, Mister?" When the figure didn't respond, she took several more steps. Perhaps he hadn't heard her. "Is everything all right? Do you need help?"

The figure stood and turned, throwing off the sopping tattered blanket he'd been wearing. He was tall and bulky as a draft horse. The gas lamp at the corner gave enough light that she could see his forearm was some kind of metal prosthesis that attached at the elbow where the metal appeared to fuse with the skin. The metal hand had large crude but functional fingers. From a distance in the dark, that arm might look like it had a cast.

Her heart started to race as Em's description of the rooftop shooter came back to her. She looked at his face. He had a patch over one eye with a long deep scar running down that cheek. Em hadn't mentioned that part.

Another whine drew her gaze back to the dog. Now that the man wasn't obscuring her view, she saw that the animal's hind legs were broken, shattered bone tearing through the skin. The puddle was red with blood. A tattered, warped slouch hat, the one he'd been wearing when Em saw him, lay next to the dog, blood soaking into the brim on the near side. She swallowed a rush of bile and stared up at the towering man in slack-jawed shock.

Water dripped from her lashes, obscuring her vision. She blinked it away. Her body vibrated with a swelling of terror. "Did… did you do that?"

He smiled. A gold tooth gleamed in the light from the corner. Several more were missing or perhaps blackened with rot. "Followed ye 'ere t'other day from that tower. Boss said ye' were like t' come back." He nodded to the dog. "Thought I'd amuse meself a bit. Gets a sight dull round 'ere."

Run. Her knees felt weak. She shook her head, unable to look away from that one bloodshot eye leering at her. She was going to be sick. "But why? What do you want with me?"

His broad shoulders lifted in a shrug. "They're payin' me to git rid of ye, not t' ask questions."

Run now. Maeko listened to the voice in her head this time. She spun around, making it a few strides before something hard struck her across the back, sending her sprawling in the wet street. The carrier flew from her hands. Grit ground into her palms when she tried to catch herself, but the force of the strike was enough that her chin hit the ground and her teeth bit into her tongue. Macak yowled, his crate hit the ground and tumbled several feet before coming to a rest upside down against the building. The coppery taste of blood filled her mouth. She struggled to get her hands and feet under her, the muscles in her upper back locked in spasm from the blow. Her stomach heaved, evacuating her scant dinner into the wet street.

A presence loomed over her, more felt than seen, like a wave crashing down. The cold metal hand closed on the back of her neck and he lifted her until her feet dangled in the air. Lights flashed behind her eyes with the pressure of his grip, the mechanical hand far stronger than any normal hand should be. The satchel slid off her shoulder and splatted in a puddle.

She tried to kick back at him, but his other arm blocked her. He grabbed her ankles with that hand and held them fast. She was little bigger than a child next to him. It wasn't fair, but life never was. Her mind raced for some way out. Pain began to cloud her thoughts. She tried to speak and choked on blood. She spit and tried again.

"Why me?" she gasped, squeezing her eyes shut against the pain of his grip.

He didn't answer. Had he even heard her? With blood pounding in her ears, would she hear him if he did answer?

She tried to scream, but her voice wouldn't come now. The mechanical hand tightened. She clawed at impervious metal with fingers that were going numb.

Tears ran from her eyes now. She couldn't stop them streaming down her cheeks along with rivulets of rain.

Em, I've found your rooftop shooter.

A loud crack rang out. Something warm spattered the back of her head. The big man sank to his knees and her toes touched ground. The hand didn't loosen. He toppled sideways then, dragging her to the street with him. Someone crouched behind her, fingers going to work on the mechanical hand, pinching her skin in their frantic scrabbling. She didn't try to help. Her arms were tired, her thoughts sluggish. Her head was jarred as someone began striking at the hand with something—metal striking metal—until it finally released. Blood rushed through. Her skull began to pound as though a thousand hammers were trying to break out from within. Her neck and back were on fire. She curled on the ground, unable to control her shaking or the tears streaming from her eyes in earnest now.

"Mae!" Chaff gathered her to his chest. "Get that bludger's body out of here and one of you put the poor mutt out of its misery. Diggs, get her things, I'm taking her inside." His hand brushed at the tears on her cheeks. "Mae, are you all right?"

She couldn't answer. The memory of the poor dog bleeding in the street filled her vision.

That could have been me.

She buried her face against his chest, eyes squeezed tight against a raging headache. Anger that he hadn't come sooner and joy that he had come at all warred inside her. The former wasn't rational. She knew that, but she let it have its say now while she was in too much pain to act on it.

He stood and carried her into the building. Minutes later, he sat her on a cot in one of several mostly intact rooms toward the back of the ramshackle building and crouched in front of her. Diggs entered the room behind them and set her things in a pile. Among them was her cap, which she hadn't even noticed had fallen off. Macak yowled, a discordant expression of displeasure now. Chaff shot a glance at the case and then up at Diggs now standing in the doorway.

"She's carrying some interesting baggage," Diggs said. "Need anything else?"

"Wait there a minute." Chaff looked at her. "We need to get you out of that jacket."

Maeko didn't move. The muscles in her back protested even the thought of movement. He began to take the jacket off for her. Pain flared in her neck, streaking up to amplify the pounding in her skull and down to flare out along her shoulders. A whimper slipped out and Chaff murmured an apology.

He took the jacket to Diggs. "Have someone clean this up and bring me a damp rag. Then go and see if anyone has something she can wear so we can get her clothes clean and dry."

The other boy nodded, but he didn't leave. "She going to be all right?" he asked in a whisper. "She took a nasty walloping out there."

"She'll be fine. You know, May, she's tough."

Ma-eh. She couldn't find her voice to correct him. A fresh flow of tears streamed down her cheeks. *Bloody fool thing to weep about.*

Diggs didn't look convinced. He stood gazing at her, hunched like a scolded puppy. "I should'a got down there faster."

Chaff put a hand on his shoulder. "You were brilliant, mate." His tone was gentle, reassuring. He was a good leader. "Go get me that wet rag so I can clean her up."

The other boy ran a hand through his hair and nodded, his shoulders still hanging when he walked away.

Chaff crouched in front of her again. "What are you doing coming around here after dark, Pigeon? I thought that rich toff was looking after you." He wiped away her tears again, but they continued to creep forth.

"Lucian's dead," she muttered. Talking made her neck hurt more, pain flaring up through her jaw and out along her shoulders.

Chaff lowered his eyes and cursed expressively under his breath. After a minute or so of tense silence, he looked at her again and squeezed her hands, making his tone once more calm and reassuring. "You do have hard luck sometimes."

Diggs returned carrying a bundle of ragtag clothes and a wet rag. Chaff took the items and ushered him out again, shutting the door behind him this time. This was Chaff's room, one of the few in the building with a door that actually shut all the way. There were some privileges to being in charge.

He set the items next to her on the cot then took a moment to open the carrier. Macak bolted over to give her a brief talking to for the rough handling then shook himself and proceeded to examine his new surroundings. Chaff shook his head, watching the smooth motion of the clockwork leg. After a few seconds staring at the exploring cat, he went to dig something out of the emergency stash he kept in a charred cabinet along one wall. He brought a small bottle over, sank down next to her and opened it, drawing out the dropper.

He held it up to her lips. "This will help."

She let her head rest back into the hand he put behind her for support. He squeezed several drops into her mouth. The fluid stung on her punctured tongue. She forced a swallow, recognizing the bitter flavor. Laudanum. Swallowing hurt too. Everything hurt.

Chaff set aside the bottle and picked up the rag. "This'll be cold, but you have some..." he screwed up his face, "bits... of that bludger on you."

Maeko's stomach did a flip, but the thought of how

much it would hurt to be sick again gave her the will to hold it back.

Chaff cleaned the back of her head as carefully as he could, apologizing whenever a moan or whimper of pain slipped out. When that was done, he helped her change clothes, keeping his gaze averted except when she needed his help. His consideration for her privacy surprised her somewhat. Many boys might have taken advantage of the moment. She wanted to thank him for his thoughtfulness, but she was too tired and sore to put the words together.

They sat on the cot again and he stayed with her. He didn't pester for answers. Instead, he stroked her hair, his touch gentle, and let her lean into him until the tincture took hold and dragged her down into sleep.

CHAPTER THIRTEEN

Maeko woke to pain and confusion. Where was she? Why did she hurt so much?

In an extreme departure from most normal mornings, she awoke laying on her side pressed against another warm body, her head pillowed on their shoulder. She held her breath and kept still, afraid of waking the other person before she figured out who they were and why she was lying with them. It took several agonizing and anxious seconds for the fog of sleep and pain to lift enough for her to recall the events of the prior day—the airship explosion, visiting Ash, the attack in the alley—and where it had all ended with her falling asleep in Chaff's protective embrace.

The initial fear making her pulse race faded, but her pulse didn't slow. One of her arms lay across his chest and she became uncomfortably aware of the lean muscle she could feel through the threadbare shirt under her hand. She liked the way he felt next to her. So warm, strong, and safe. This would add another layer of complication to her troubled relationships, but at least both of them were fully dressed.

Macak curled against her low back, making a blazing hot spot there, almost as hot as her face felt while she tried to think of some way to extricate herself from her well-surrounded position without waking Chaff.

A small shift of her hip to try to budge the cat sent spasms through her injured back, which sent a spasm through her neck in turn and wrenched a cry from her. Chaff shifted, placing a hand on her arm. So much for not waking him.

"Are you all right?"

Pain still blazed like white hot fire through her back and she felt warm tears slip free of her eyes. She muttered a few curses under her breath.

Chaff shifted his shoulder out so her head now rested on his arm and turned on his side to face her. She didn't dare try to move again yet, not knowing how much the effort would hurt. He brushed away a tear with his thumb. He looked so very concerned and he was so very close.

She felt a little lightheaded now and it wasn't only from pain. *Blast his worried blue eyes. I'm in no shape to be swooning over a boy.* The tight, painful muscles in her neck discouraged jaw movement, so she spoke in a whisper. "I was trying to get up without disturbing you."

Chaff smiled. He did have a lovely smile. It was beautiful to see after all she'd been through.

"Stubborn bird. You got done down hard. You need to let me help you."

She clenched her jaw and winced at the resulting lance of pain.

Chaff chuckled at her thwarted defiance. "Will you let me help you?"

She started to nod and ended up squeezing her eyes shut against more tears.

He kissed her forehead. "How could anyone not love you?" he murmured and started to climb out of the cot over her and Macak.

Her heart stuttered and her eyes popped open. What was that he said? No, she wasn't going to think about it. She couldn't, not right now. Thinking about it made her headache worse.

Macak hopped off the cot with a squeak of protest at Chaff's prodding. Then he helped her up, doing most of the work so she wouldn't have to engage her injured muscles any more than necessary. The process ended up being a painful one despite both their efforts to avoid hurting her and more of those irritating tears slipped free. She'd had about enough of those.

"You need more laudanum?"

She shook her head, regretted it, and decided whispering her responses might be the better option. "Not yet. I need to visit the privy."

"Do you need help?"

She gave him a sharp look.

"I didn't mean..." He chuckled and went to open the door, sweeping a hand in front of him to usher her on her way. "Go on then. I should've known you'd be too bloody stubborn to let me help you."

She walked to the door, every step sending a spasm through her back no matter how deliberate and careful she tried to be.

He leaned close as she went past, a glimmer of amusement breaking through the concern in his eyes. "You'll be pressing me for that laudanum by the time you get back."

She thought about cursing him, but it would take far too much of the energy she needed for walking. Settling for a glare out of the corner of her eye, she made her laborious way out into the building.

Many of the boys who were up and moving around in the chaotic array of salvaged furniture and makeshift living areas she recognized. Their greetings were friendly enough, in the manner of comrades under one leadership, though Chaff was more of a mentor than a leader to many of them. Some winced in sympathy for her obvious pain and some gave suggestive winks toward Chaff's room that she might have slugged them for under different circumstances.

Macak trotted along beside her, taking his self-appointed responsibility as her escort very seriously and earning several comments and appraising looks as he pranced through the hideout, his clockwork leg gleaming in the light of myriad lanterns and candles.

How dusty and ragged it all looked after her brief stay with Lucian. And the smell... Best not to focus too much on that. Suffice it to say that she kind of missed the dreadful perfume Constance was always trying to put on her.

By the time she made her slow progression back to Chaff's room, she did want to beg for more laudanum and perhaps for him to carry her the last several steps to the cot as well. Chaff might never let her live that down though, so she trudged the last little bit across the room to the cot while he watched with one eyebrow cocked, expecting the call for help to come at any moment.

She stopped next to the cot and stared down at it. Chaff clicked the door shut behind Macak. She tried to sink down gracefully, but it turned into more of a fall. By the time she righted herself to sit on the edge of the cot amidst numerous pained gasps and more tears, Chaff was standing there holding up a mixture of beer and laudanum tincture.

She accepted the offered drink, gagging on the bitter aftertaste and the sting as it ran over her wounded tongue. She watched him put the bottle away. "I never got off a scream. How did you know I was in trouble last night?"

Chaff dunked a rag in a small basin of water and came to sit next to her. He placed the cold rag against her neck. It felt good, relieving some of the burning ache there. She closed her eyes and leaned into him.

Macak curled up on her other side against her hip and began to purr. She stroked his head, the contentment of his furry warm body on one side and Chaff's strong comforting presence on the other lifting her mood a touch despite the pain.

"I figured the coin purse you sent meant we were still safe here. Nice job nicking that when I was distracted, by the way," he added with a sly grin. "However, I still don't trust that detective bird, so I set some of the boys on extra watches just in case. Diggs was on rooftop watch when he saw that bludger attack you. Creepy bloke had been lurking around for a bit. Diggs ran down fast as he could, grabbing me and a few other boys on the way. The bloke must have been on something. Diggs and I both hit him from behind with boards that'd come off the building. Didn't do so much as distract him from you, so Diggs grabbed the bludger's side iron and shot him in the back of the head. Right powerful piece he had too, unmarked with a wicked kick that set Diggs back on his arse in the dirt. The bloke didn't even seem to notice he'd been shot for a second."

She stared at the tattered remains of a carpet near the bed. "He's dead."

"And gone."

Mostly gone. She'd be surprised if they hadn't taken his mechanical arm for the value of the parts at the very least.

Chaff brushed her hair back from her face with careful fingers. She hadn't cut it quite short enough the last time. Already the front was growing out to the point that it hung into her eyes. His hand slid around the side of her face, brushing along her cheek, tracing her jaw. In that moment, she thought she understood why cats loved being petted so much. She managed a weary smile.

"I didn't know if we were going to get him off you in time."

The tightness in his voice caught her attention and she opened her eyes, but her injured neck wouldn't let her turn to look at him. She let the laudanum and his light caress lull her eyes shut again. He flipped the rag against her neck, turning it to a cooler section. She almost drifted off before he spoke again.

"That arm of his... I've never seen anything like it. It was almost like that cat's leg, only clumsier and not finished off so nice."

"That cat's name is Macak," she muttered.

Macak made a soft chirrup sound in recognition of his name then went back to purring.

"So it seems." Chaff set the rag aside and moved away, keeping a hand on her shoulder to hold her upright. "Mae."

He said her name right, that meant this was important. She forced her eyes open against the weight of laudanum dragging them down. He had knelt in front of her, his eyes bright with worry.

"Do you know who he was, that bludger in the ally with the metal arm?"

The question had to come. She'd expected it before this. She tried to draw in a deep steadying breath, but her lungs were heavy and her back hurt. She settled for a small inhale. It didn't clear her head as much as she would have liked. "He is... was... one of the men who killed Commissioner Henderson."

Chaff lowered his gaze. The muscles in his jaw worked, clenching and unclenching. The news upset him, as it should. This mess was big on a scale that went well above the business of the streets. She felt bad about involving him in it. This wasn't his trouble. To be fair, she hadn't realized it was hers either until the big brute said as much. Whoever took out the commissioner wanted her gone too for some reason. It might be nothing more than her association with Em, but she had also been living with Lucian when the commissioner visited, so there was no way to know for sure without talking to whoever was behind it all. Trouble was, whoever they were, they didn't seem much interested in talking.

"I don't suppose it was a coincidence that he came after you?"

Fear kindled inside her, twisting her gut into so many knots. Would Chaff want her to leave if she told him the truth? A lot of boys counted on him for a safe haven off the streets. Her presence threatened that.

She had to force the words out through sudden constriction in her throat. "No. He said someone paid him to get rid of me. I don't know who or why exactly."

He was silent a long time, staring at Macak. Fear swelled in her, pushing out against the insistent calm brought on by the laudanum. It would be too dangerous to let her stay. The only sensible thing to do would be to send her away, but she didn't want to be on her own again, not yet. Much as she hated to admit it, she needed him.

"You should get some rest," he murmured.

"No. I need to check the papers."

Chaff shook his head, a wry smile drawing up the corners of his mouth a fraction. "You need to heal. I'll go scout out the news."

He slid a hand around into her hair then and she closed her eyes, relaxing into the touch and savoring the relief that he didn't seem to be in a hurry to send her away quite yet. The touch of his lips, slightly parted and soft against hers, caught her by surprise. The kiss was gentle, mindful of her injuries. Her pulse began to race, waging a new war against the sedating effect of the drug. The conflict made her dizzy and breathless.

He was her friend, her mentor, at times even her rival, not... not this, and yet she dreaded the moment he would pull away. She needed his help, but that wasn't all she wanted anymore. The touch of his lips stirred other wants.

Their lips moved apart a fraction. He was breathing faster now. His hand slid forward to caress her cheek. For several seconds, he stayed there as if torn, his breath tickling her lips. He kissed her again, lightly and without lingering this time, then shifted back and stood, turning away from her. The room spun. She swallowed and resisted the impulse to call him back.

"Get some rest. I'll bring some eats back with me." He sounded tense, a spring wound to the point of breaking.

"There's some tin in my coin purse," she whispered.

He nodded and picked up the purse from the pile in the corner, moving some of the coin into his pocket before slipping silent from the room. She stared at the door for a several minutes wishing there were some way to know what he was thinking before she gave up and eased herself down on her side. The way her pulse still raced, she didn't think she would sleep much, but the laudanum worked its magic and she drifted off, Macak a tiny heater curled against her chest.

When she woke again, the door was cracked and Macak was gone. She got the feeling she'd been asleep a long time, though the light in this part of the building rarely changed. There were hushed voices outside the door, two people having a quiet conversation she couldn't quite make out. With great care, she sat up, feeling a smidgen more mobile than before. Chaff walked in, no doubt alerted by the creaking of the cot. Macak trotted in with him and he closed the door. He set some things on the cabinet then placed his hands on the corners and leaned into them, not looking at her.

She touched a finger to her lips, remembering the kiss. He was quite good at it, at least in her limited experience. Did he regret doing it? Did she?

"How many girls have you kissed?" She bit the inside of her lip as soon as the words were out. What kind of question was that? How did that matter at all next to everything else that was going on?

He froze for a telling second, then answered, "Just you."

Her chest tightened. "Don't lie."

"Just you... recently." He dug the remaining coins out of his pocket and dropped them on the cabinet top. "Do you really want to talk about this?"

He appeared tenser now than when he'd left. Had something happened while she was sleeping to upset him? If so, she would do him the courtesy of giving him time to bring it up when he was ready, especially since her wits hadn't fully recovered from the lingering effects of the laudanum, as proven by that ridiculous question.

"I was only curious."

"Why, because I'm good at it?" He gave her a quick sideways glance and almost smiled before turning to back stare at the coins on the cabinet again.

"Yes." She felt her cheeks flush with the admission.

"You know I've spent my whole life on the streets."

"What does that mean?"

"It's come up a few times."

She couldn't stop herself from stumbling further down that path. "Kissing?"

"That is what we were taking about." He sounded almost angry now.

Was that jealousy twisting in her gut or hunger pangs? Something in the things he'd set down smelled delicious and it was making her mouth water. She would assume it was only hunger. Still...

"Maybe I shouldn't sleep in here."

He spun to face her, pushing away from the cabinet hard enough that the top rocked back and bumped the wall, scattering coins and other items. "Maybe you shouldn't be here at all."

CHAPTER FOURTEEN

Maeko stared. Her throat tightened. She could think of nothing to say. Had she done something to make Chaff angry? Was he finally realizing the risk? Was she about to be booted to the street?

"I'm confused about something. You said Lucian was dead." He pointed in the vague direction of the main exit from the building. "The papers say it was Mr. Folesworth's twin brother who died in that airship explosion. You need to tell me what's really going on. This isn't a game. Everyone here may be in danger."

She should have explained all of that by now, but pain and laudanum had muddled her thoughts. His advances hadn't helped with that either so, in a sense, he also shared some blame for the inadequate communication. She considered pointing that out, but the fire in his eyes was sufficient discouragement. "Mr. Folesworth's twin brother did die in the explosion, just not the brother everyone thinks. Thaddeus is trying to take Lucian's place as the head of Clockwork Enterprises."

This was the first time she could ever remember seeing him turn that pale when he wasn't sick or grievously injured.

He shifted his stance and started to speak then fell silent, his arm dropping back to his side. His brow furrowed and his narrowed eyes darted about with the flurry of racing thoughts. Several seconds passed before he looked at her, or more like through her, and asked, "You're certain?"

"Yes."

He began to pace, muscles in his jaw jumping with the grinding of his teeth. Macak darted out of his path and hopped up to settle behind her on the cot.

"This is a sorry and sad mess, Pigeon."

She responded with a tiny nod, struggling with the tears that stung her eyes. Bollocks, she'd had enough of tears, but... he believed her. He didn't like it any more than she did, but he was taking her at her word.

Chaff stopped by the wall and stared at nothing for several uncomfortable minutes. He nodded after a bit. "I should have the boys move to a different lurk here in town." Finally, he faced her again. "You and I can head out to the place in Whitechapel."

His words didn't reconcile with what she was expecting him to say. Had she heard him right? "You and I?"

He gave her a pained look. "Did you think I would just kick you to the streets?"

She stared at him. Perhaps she really hadn't woken up yet. This was some dream she was having about how she wanted things to work out. "I... Yes, I did. That's what you should do."

He grimaced. "Maybe so, but that's not what I intend to do."

She might have kissed him then, had she the ability to stand up before second thoughts crept in. Pain kept her from such spontaneity, which was probably best. He didn't need any encouragement.

"I'll have Diggs start moving the boys out. We'll have everyone out of here by tomorrow night. You can take one more day to rest and recover, then we'll head out too." He turned toward the door, ready to get moving on his plan.

"Chaff."

He faced her again, looking smug and expectant.

"Maybe I shouldn't sleep in here tonight."

He chuckled wryly. "Here I thought maybe you were about to apologize for bringing this chaos down on our merry den of thieves." His playful wink lightened the hard truth within his words, but his expression was sober when he continued. "Pigeon, the boys don't care where you sleep. You need a quiet place to rest and this room is the best place in the building for that. Besides, I can't take care of you as well if you're not here."

Or do any number of other things you might be of a mind to try? She let it go. It took too much effort to argue.

He nodded as if the subject were resolved and strode from the room, a man with a mission.

While he was gone, she made short work of the meal he'd brought her. With food in her stomach, she felt strong enough to wander around the building for a short time to stretch her legs and chat with some of the other thieves and pickpockets residing there. Most of them she knew, though the boy she'd chased down the other day scowled and moved off when she came near. They all still found Macak fascinating and the cat basked in the attention.

None of them mentioned the sleeping arrangements, though a few knowing glances passed between some of the older boys. Perhaps they really didn't care what she and Chaff did behind closed doors, not that they had done anything. The boys also didn't appear to care that she had brought this upheaval upon them. Moving around to stay out of Literati hands was part of their life. It didn't matter so much what the catalyst was. They were used to it.

Diggs and Chaff went around the building, hurrying some boys along in their departure preparations and doling out orders on who would leave when so there wasn't a conspicuous mass exodus from the building. It was good that Chaff had Diggs to back him up. She had always tried to be helpful in that regard, but, while those who knew her respected her skills, most of them still weren't keen to take direction from a girl. They would listen to Diggs.

When the ache in her back and neck became too intense again, she trudged back to the room. Chaff was there ahead of her sorting through the cabinet and tossing things into a satchel to take with them. The clothes Em had given her lay folded on top of Macak's carrier.

He closed the cabinet and set the satchel aside when she entered. "How are you feeling?"

She recalled a comment Thaddeus had made and smiled bitterly. "Like I was run over by a hansom."

"That good." He smiled sympathetically as he stood and walked over to her. "Let me take a look at your back."

She hesitated a moment, then turned her back to him and unbuttoned the top several buttons of the shirt, shifting it all up to keep her front covered while giving him enough slack to pull the collar down and see her back. Chaff shifted the collar around and whistled softly.

"He did you down real good, Pigeon." His fingers pressed lightly on one spot and she sucked in a sharp breath. "Sorry. Do you think anything's broken?"

"Hurt's like the blazes, but I don't think so. How does it look?"

"Like the skin of a rotten pear, just like your neck where he squeezed it."

She turned her head a little to smirk over her shoulder at him, delighted that her neck let her get away with that much motion and that talking hurt a little less now than it had. "Thanks. That makes me feel so much better." She faced forward again, feeling the beginnings of a spasm in her neck.

"How does it feel here?"

His soft voice triggered an alarm, but she didn't have a chance to react before his lips touched her neck. A shiver went through her, setting off a blaze of pain in her back and neck that killed any pleasure she might have gotten from it. She cried out and twisted away. His face, when she turned on him, was almost comical with guilt and surprise, though she wasn't feeling especially amused. She gave him a frosty look and began to button up the shirt.

"I'm sorry. You know I wouldn't hurt you on purpose." He was trying hard not to smile, which didn't please her. "I honestly didn't expect that much of a reaction."

"I'm sleeping somewhere else," she grumbled.

"May."

She glared daggers at him and he winced as if stung.

"Mae," he corrected. "I promise I won't try anything else." He held up his hands in a show of surrender. "Let me take care of you tonight. I'll make sure there's a separate room for you in the place at Whitechapel if that's what you want."

Did he mean that, or was he just trying to appease her for now? Most likely the latter, though she gave a small nod, accepting the terms at face value for simplicity sake. They could have a row about it if necessary when they got there and she'd healed a little more.

"You should take some laudanum or you won't get any sleep tonight."

"I slept most of the day away," she protested. She was sick of being in pain and sick of being coddled.

"And more rest will help you heal."

"You're not my Mum," she snapped.

"You think she'd say any differently?"

She didn't answer. Her estranged mother was still providing illegal medical care to the Pirates, even after Lucian paid off her debt as part of his show of gratitude for Maeko's role in saving his life. Her mother would, without a doubt, agree with Chaff on this. In fact, she would probably ask him to hold her down so she could ladle the foul liquid down Maeko's throat.

"I thought so." Chaff shook his head at her. "Stubborn bird."

He dug the bottle out while she continued to scowl at him. Right or not, he would at least know that she wasn't happy about it. He mixed some into a cup. She grabbed it from him and swallowed it, then threw the cup back at him. He caught it and grinned, putting the cup and the laudanum in the satchel.

When the drug began to take effect, he sat next to her on the cot and put a cold rag against her neck again to ease the pain and swelling. She tried to stay aware and apart, but it was wasted effort. In time, she sank into him and drifted to sleep.

•

Despite her best intentions, she woke the next morning pressed against him with Macak curled at her feet, only this time Chaff had gotten rid of his shirt at some point. She didn't recall when, but she did recall the incidents that led to many of the scars on his chest and abdomen. Most were from knife fights and an unfortunate number of those had been the result of his coming to her defense. He always had tried to take care of her. Perhaps it shouldn't surprise her that he insisted on doing so now.

When she ran away at the age of seven, she thought the harsh realities of life in the brothel had forced her to grow up fast, but ten-year-old Chaff had amazed her.

He understood the streets and the laws that governed there and, most importantly, how to use them to his advantage, better than any of the adults she'd run into. Yet, with all his street smarts, he could be so frustratingly immature at times. It had taken her a while to discover that was more a boy thing than a Chaff thing.

A faint smile turned her lips and her gaze wandered down to a puckered scar a few inches below his ribcage. That had been the end result of someone offering to buy her for a night when she was eleven. Even as a gangly fourteen year old, he could come out on top of most single battles. The other bloke had fled the scene in worse condition, but the wound had infected later and almost killed Chaff. The recollection of those tense days, terrified that he would die because of her, made her throat clench. Her hand slid down, drawn by memories, her fingers tracing the edge of the scar.

His breathing changed suddenly and his hand came up, catching her wrist in an iron grip. "I know you're in no shape for the reaction that kind of touching is going to get you right now."

Bound up desire in his voice brought a hot burn to her cheeks.

"I... I was just remembering when that happened."

After a few seconds, his grip on her wrist loosened. He slid his hand up to take hold of hers, guiding it to a long thin scar over his heart. "Remember this one?"

She couldn't stop a smile. "Yes. That was when you were teaching me how to defend myself with a blade."

He chuckled. "You took to it a little faster than I expected."

Macak, not wanting to be left out of the conversation, climbed up onto Chaff's chest and sat there, staring down at both of them. Drawn by the irresistible power of feline expectation, they both started to pet him. He lifted his head, inviting a scratch on his white chin, which Maeko obliged. Chaff stopped petting and poked at the metal paw.

"Quite the contraption. You couldn't have made off with a less conspicuous cat? He'll never fit in with the strays around Whitechapel."

She grinned. "He wanted to come."

"Can't say I blame him. Given the choice between you and a sibling-slaughtering mad man I'd probably choose you too."

"Probably?" She poked him in the ribs and he twisted away. Macak rode out the motion, digging in his claws.

"Ouch! He's almost as prickly as you, Pigeon." Chaff lifted the cat then. "And right now he needs to chivvy along. Those claws are sharp and that metal is really cold on bare skin. Besides, I need to go make sure things are proceeding as planned." He set Macak down above his head and got up, helping her up with him. Then he picked up her clothes from on top of the carrier and handed them to her. "I imagine you'll want to change back into those. Which reminds me." He turned his back and began putting on his shirt while he spoke. She took the cue, standing and putting her back to him while she swapped shirts as fast as her sore back would allow. "Where'd you get those togs? I didn't get the impression Mr. Folesworth was the type to dress a bird in boy's clothes."

"Em."

"The detective?"

She caught the edge in his voice and an ominous stillness fell over the room, as if they all waited for something, like an explosion. Here was another thing she probably should have mentioned up front. Now that she thought about it, was today the day she was supposed to meet Em again?

"Yes. The detective."

"Care to explain why she'd be doing you a favor like that? She didn't strike me as the generous type."

"She's definitely not. It wasn't a favor." She glanced around to make sure he wasn't looking then changed out her trousers.

"I had a feeling. What did you do for her?"

"I gave her information. The night he was snuffed, the commissioner met with Lucian. Em's investigating his death or Lucian's involvement with him. Or maybe she's still following up on the incident with his partner. I'm not exactly sure." Something she needed to clarify when she met with the detective again, though she didn't know how or when that would be under the circumstances.

"Didn't we have a talk about communication when I first took you under my wing?"

She finished fastening the trousers and turned around. He was already facing her and his wicked smirk made her wonder exactly how long he'd been looking. "Yes. I believe your exact words were 'you tell me everything, Pigeon, and I'll tell you what you need to know'."

There was a knock on the door. He gave her his dashing scoundrel grin and reached for the handle. "That sounds about right."

She threw a balled up sock at him as he opened the door. It bounced off his cheek and Diggs caught it.

Diggs chuckled and tossed it back at her. "Good to see you're feeling more like yourself, Mae."

She caught the sock. "Morning, Diggs."

"How're things going?" Chaff asked.

"Exactly as planned, excepting I found some grumpy harlot in men's clothes sneaking round the building. Says she's looking for Maeko."

Chaff gave her a meaningful glance. "Talk of the devil..."

aeko tucked the remaining contents of her coin purse into an inside pocket of her jacket, then she and Chaff followed Diggs back out to the more devastated front section of the building where he had left Em waiting. Diggs stopped at the doorway into the room, letting Maeko approach the detective with Chaff hanging a few steps behind. It was a bit like having a guard, which didn't seem an out of place thought since neither boy looked overly happy about the woman's presence.

Maeko ignored the challenging glances the two exchanged with Em. "I thought we were supposed to meet later today?"

Em smirked. "And you were going to show up for that, were you?"

"I don't know. Things have changed."

"Just a little," Em answered, prickly as usual. "It took me a while to confirm that you'd left the flat after the airship incident without drawing attention to myself. I figured you would have come back to this." Her eyes swept the broken down room and the two boys with open disdain.

Chaff stepped forward to stand at Maeko's shoulder.

"This is where I belong. Did you come here to insult my friends and me or do we have business to conduct?"

"There are a number of developments since the explosion that I find curious. I hoped you might be able to shed some light on them. And I thought you might like to know that Captain Garrett and two of his band have been arrested in connection with the airship explosion."

Maeko's mouth went dry. "What about Ash?"

Em glanced at Chaff with a knowing smirk and Maeko winced inwardly. The question had simply popped out. Perhaps she should have waited to get Em alone before asking, though, from where she was standing, Chaff's expression still looked stone cold, his eyes not leaving the detective.

"They haven't arrested the two boys. Although they aren't done with the investigation yet. I have some important things to talk to you about. Can we go somewhere private?" Em pointed to the exit.

Somewhere private like her coach, which would put her at the woman's mercy. If she went, Chaff would be upset, but it would give her the opportunity to check in on Ash and get Em's input on the situation. The detective might have a miserable attitude most of the time, but her experience could prove useful.

She looked up at Chaff who eventually left off glaring at Em to meet her gaze. Resistance blazed like an out of control house fire in his eyes.

"I need to go with Em. Just for a bit."

His eyes narrowed. "You're in no shape to be out adventuring."

"I have to do this. Please trust me."

His shoulders stiffened and he leaned a few inches away from her. Not an encouraging sign. "I do trust you. One of the things I trust you to do best is get yourself into trouble."

Em chuckled. "He may not be as dumb as he looks."

Maeko threw an arm out to stop Chaff's sudden

advance, grinding her teeth against the pain the sudden gesture caused. Diggs also moved into the room, ready to intervene, though she wasn't entirely sure on whose behalf.

She gave Em a piercing look. "Can you leave us alone for a minute?"

Em shrugged. "I'll be outside."

When she was gone, Diggs turned and vanished back deeper into the building, also leaving them alone. The tension in the room swelled the moment the others were gone.

She met Chaff's eyes and started to speak, but he put a finger to her lips, his touch gentle despite the anger she saw in his eyes.

"You're hurt and there could be others like that bludger out looking for you. You know this is a bad idea."

So many arguments went through her mind, all of them things he could counter easily enough. The bottom line was that she wanted to check on Ash and she wanted, deep down, to see Thaddeus suffer for what he'd done, assuming, of course that she wasn't wrong about everything, but now wasn't the time for self-doubt. If she went into hiding with Chaff, Thaddeus would probably give up on her after a while, but he would also get everything he wanted. As least if Em knew the truth, there was a small chance that something might be done about it.

"Yes. I know it's a bad idea, but I'm going to do it anyway and you know that."

He closed his eyes for a quick second and took a deep breath. "I'm not letting you get hurt again."

"You know that isn't in your hands, Chaff. You can't keep me safe from myself." Macak, who had been hanging back, now sauntered over and wound through her legs, making it easier for her to force a smile and hide the pain it brought her to see such torment in his eyes. "I'll meet you in Whitechapel tonight."

He wanted to argue, she could see it in the set of his jaw, the tension in his shoulders, the white knuckles of his fist. Instead, he released the fist and brought a hand up to her cheek. A flutter rose in her stomach. The butterflies were back, but it wasn't fear that called them in this time. He stepped in and kissed her, his hand on her cheek trembling with pent up emotion. This time she shifted closer, ignoring the pain, and kissed him in return, as much to savor the heady sensation of that contact as to thank him for letting her win, because he was going to let her win.

Delicious warmth flooded through her, a pleasure so intoxicating she slid one hand around the back of his neck to keep him there. Her lips parted slightly when his did and his tongue slipped between them. She tensed, letting out a tiny squeak of surprise. His other hand came to rest on her hip and pulled her body against his. The brief flare of pain in her back wasn't enough to make her want the moment to end. The longer they kissed, the more she wanted be closer to him. She opened her mouth a little more, exploring and tasting him, delighting in the feel of his body pressed against her. A flood of longing heated her, the pounding of her heart drowning out thought.

He drew back, ending the kiss, and rested his forehead against hers, his eyes closed. It took her a few seconds to get her balance again. They were both breathing hard.

"If you need me, I'll be here until tonight to see that all the boys get moved out."

"Can I leave Macak with you for now?"

He nodded. "Be careful," he murmured.

She took hold of the hand that still rested on her hip, surprised by how much she didn't want to walk away, and made herself step back from him. He looked perfect standing there in the midst of the broken down building, strong and lean, a hunger in his eyes burning for her. He wanted Maeko the street rat. The little half-Asian pickpocket whose every flaw he already knew. It was flattering in a way she wasn't used to, but what surprised her more was how much she reciprocated that feeling.

"I will." She squeezed his hand then loosened her grip, letting their hands slide apart. "Ganbatte."

"Ganbatte."

•

Em watched with her shrewd gaze as Maeko climbed gingerly into the coach. She sat on the edge of the seat and met the detective's questioning look. The coach began to move at the customary knock on the roof from Em.

"It doesn't take skilled sleuthing to see that you're in a considerable amount of pain."

Was that a hint of concern in the cold woman's voice? With the lingering inner glow from her parting with Chaff bolstering her mood, it was all she could do not to make a jesting comment on that, but she didn't want to brass Em off. "I found your rooftop shooter. He put a fine effort into crushing the life out of me." She told Em all about the man's strange arm and what he'd said about being paid to kill her.

"I'll assume you didn't sweet talk your way out of that encounter."

Maeko shivered, all too aware of how close she'd come to dying, and gritted her teeth against a flare of pain. "No. The bludger's dead. Chaff and Diggs had to kill him to get him off me."

Em nodded, her expression grim. "My only solid

lead to the man who actually killed the commissioner." Then her eyes lit and she smiled. "Then again, if someone wants you dead, I imagine they'll send someone else after you soon enough."

Another shiver almost pulled a groan from her. She swallowed it back. "Brilliant," Maeko grumbled.

"Here, what do you make of this?" Em picked up some newspapers from the seat next to her and handed them across.

The cover of one was all about unnamed suspects arrested for the murder of Thaddeus Folesworth. The cover of the next one made her feel sick.

> Joel Jacard, business partner to Lucian Folesworth, founder of Clockwork Enterprises, was released from custody today upon the discovery of evidence clearing his name in the murder case of Anna and Elizabeth Folesworth. Mr. Jacard explained that his perceived abduction of Mr. Folesworth was a panicked attempt to protect his longtime friend and business partner from the people coming after him. Mr. Folesworth, still coping with the death of his wife and daughter as well as the recent tragic loss of his brother, was present at the release. The two men embraced one another in a heartwarming display of forgiveness and understanding.

She looked up at Em. "Is this real?"

"Odd, isn't it. His brother dies and now he's publicly embracing the man who murdered his family. Of course, there is always the possibility that Mr. Jacard didn't kill them."

Her jaw dropped. All the good feelings were gone now. "How can you say that? You were there in the warehouse. You saw what Joel was like."

Em started to speak when the coach jerked to a stop.

They moved as one to the window and drew back the curtains.

A couple of younger men were on the corner ahead of them with stacks of newspapers. They held copies out to passers and bellowed into the crowd. "Get your Pirate Journal! The Literati aim to make slaves of the working man! Read all about it here! Find out who really killed Commissioner Henderson and why!"

Traffic had stopped because four Literati officers were in the street brandishing their clubs and trying to outshout the Pirate newsboys, ordering them to cease distributing their lies or be taken into custody. The men not only ignored the shouting, but raised their own voices further still and were joined by three burly blokes who came to stand between them and the officers.

Maeko cracked the door and leaned out for a better view.

One officer swapped his club out for his gun. A fourth bloke joined the men standing between the Lits and the Pirate newsboys. The officer fired his gun into the air. Several horses startled and most of the passing pedestrians cried out, spreading away from the conflict like water rippling away from a dropped stone.

"We've a right to be here," one of the Pirates shouted.

"Not anymore you don't," an officer snarled back.

One of the big blokes in the middle swung his meaty fist out, catching the officer in the jaw. That was the signal for everything to fall apart. The officer with the gun out fired on the bloke. The man's hands went to his chest and he fell back into one of the men with the papers who also fell, the stack of papers scattering across the pavement. The other man passing out papers threw his handful aside and tackled the officer with the gun. The rest of the men and another officer dove into the fray. Some of the crowd crept near, fascinated by violence, while others fled the area.

Maeko stepped out of the coach. Em grabbed after her, fingers coming close enough to brush her arm as she darted over and snatched up a paper from the ground. With that in hand, she dashed back to the coach, wincing when another gunshot fired and woman in front of the clockmaker's shop screamed, red blooming bright across the pale ivory of her bodice. Maeko's eyes met hers for a moment, then the woman sank to her knees and wavered there a few seconds before crumpling to the ground.

Maeko froze, a painful knot forming in her throat, until the massive steam powered clock above the shop exhaled, jarring her back to herself. She ducked into the coach, her back and neck on fire with pain from the brief flurry of activity. When the door was shut and Em sat back in her seat scowling at her, Maeko peeked out the window again.

The last shot had finished what the first started. Two of the big men were dragging their wounded comrade away. Both of the men who'd been distributing papers were on the ground in cuffs with a Lit officer standing over them. Two officers had gone to the aide of the wounded woman who lay unmoving before the shop. The last officer gathered the strewn papers in a pile and lit them on fire there on the pavement.

A clacking sound drew Maeko's gaze up to the headline boards on either side of the big steam clock. When the letters on one side finished flipping it read, LITERATI, FOR A BRIGHTER FUTURE.

Indeed. She snapped the curtains closed, feeling naught but disgust for the lot of them. Perhaps this was what fed Em's bitterness. Watching innocents hurt and killed in a fight they wanted no part of. Was there a right side?

Em watched her with a bitter gaze while she flipped through the short paper. "You need to be more careful."

Maeko shrugged off her anger, wincing at yet another flash of pain in her back. "You wanted to look at it too."

Em turned away to stare through a fine line of light streaming between the curtains. "What does it say?"

"It claims the Lits are trying to enslave the working class. Also says that powerful Literati officials hired someone to kill the commissioner. They're calling for the people to fight back." Maeko set it down on the seat. "Nothing unexpected."

"Brilliant. Encourage the unarmed common folk to incite the wrath of the people with the big guns. Typical Pirate rubbish."

The coach finally started moving again. Maeko resisted the nagging urge to look out and see if the woman by the shop was alive. She would imagine they had saved her. It was easier that way.

CHAPTER SIXTEEN

E m's grey eyes shone in the light from the window when she turned back to Maeko. "Back to the business at hand. Why would Mr. Folesworth welcome Joel back after all that's happened if the man killed his family?"

"It makes perfect sense, unfortunately." Several things clicked together in Maeko's head then and unhappy certainty made her cold. "Back when I first told Lucian about you, when he was still in hiding, he thought it odd that his brother had hired a woman detective to find him. He said Thaddeus didn't have much respect for professional women. Maybe he hired a woman because he expected you to fail. Maybe Thaddeus and Joel have been working together to get Lucian out of the way this whole time."

"How does that make sense if Thaddeus died in…?" She trailed off, her eyes widening. "You think Lucian died in that explosion."

"I do. I saw them together. They're perfect twins. Lucian was a private man. All Joel and Thaddeus had to do is eliminate the people closest to him, his wife and daughter most importantly, and, given his recent losses, even if someone did notice something, they aren't apt to question him. Who's going to argue that Thaddeus isn't Lucian?"

Other than me, of course. Which meant there would almost certainly be others coming after her. *I should have stayed with Chaff.*

Em grimaced and rubbed at her temples as if her head hurt. "If that's true, then they may be cleaning house. There's been no public mention of Lucian taking you in and, after that bloke tried to kill you, I think we can confidently say that someone intends for you to disappear. Garrett and his band were suspects in the previous mess. That sets them up rather nicely to take the fall for all of this. I'm also starting to think it was more than just coincidence that those men took shots at my team the other night. If all this is true, your friend Ash may be in danger too."

And there was one of the major reasons she hadn't stayed with Chaff. Maeko rubbed her eyes. Her head hurt now too. "You said they hadn't picked him up yet?"

"No, but what I left out earlier was that they didn't pick him up because the Lits haven't located Garrett's wife and her two sons yet."

Maeko chewed her lip for a moment. "Then Ash must have given Captain Garrett my warning. He sent them away in case he couldn't smooth things over with Mr. Folesworth."

Em's smile was smug. "So you did warn them. I thought as much."

"Of course I did. I wouldn't be much of a friend otherwise."

"You and Ash are only friends then? You'd rather give your affection to that Chaff boy?"

Maeko scowled at her.

"That boy's trouble. He'll never be on the right side of the law. If you want my advice—"

"I don't."

"Suit yourself." She shrugged and moved on without missing a beat. "If Thaddeus really has stepped into his brother's shoes, then he must be working with the Literati on something big. We already know Lits were involved in the incident with Joel and they have plenty of reason to want the commissioner dead. He pleaded with the queen to be given back the jurisdictions the Lits pushed the Bobbies out of and apparently tried to get in through the back door with Lucian Folesworth. His meddling threatened their control of the city. The Pirates are probably right to point a finger that way. If only we could get our hands on the other shooter." Em smiled again. "Perhaps what we need is bait."

Maeko hated it when she smiled. It usually meant something bad for someone else. "I am not getting shot for your investigation."

"If we play it right, you won't have to. We just need to draw the shooter out to where I can get my hands on him."

"No. This is way above my head. You can keep your tin. I'm leaving the area for a while."

"Are you? You're not worried about your friend Ash?" Em began to clean her nails with a small dagger she pulled out of her long coat.

Maeko considered grabbing it. Perhaps she could use it to poke out the haughty look in the woman's eyes. The worst thing was, she did care. She had to take the bait. "What do you know?"

"Help me find the shooter."

"This is blackmail and I can find Ash if I need to through my network on the streets."

Em glanced at her out of the corner of her eye, feigning disinterest. "How fast can you find him? Will it be fast enough to help him?"

Maeko glared at her. Could she find him fast enough? Probably not as fast as if she just got the information from Em. Still, she'd almost been killed by one of these men already, was this a good enough reason to give another one a go at it? "Why can't you be the bait?"

"Because we're not sure I'm a target. We both know you are."

"Bloody hell," she snarled. "I'll help you find the shooter. Would it kill you ask nicely at least?"

"Nice gets you nowhere, Rat. I'd expect you to know that by now." Em knocked on the front wall of the coach.

A panel slid open through which Maeko could see the back of the driver's head. He turned his ear to the opening.

"Take us to the house," Em ordered.

The driver nodded and Em slid the panel shut. Rain began to pound down on the roof of the carriage, the kind of rain that clogged gutters and made mires out of unpaved streets. It suited Maeko's mood. She rode along in morose silence, flipping through the papers. There were mentions of numerous other clashes between Literati and Pirates, most resulting in bystander injuries and a few fatalities. Something on the last page of one caught her eye. It was a small side article.

Clockwork Enterprises has entered negotiations to secure funding for development and testing of several weapon prototypes designed by the company's founder, Lucian P. Folesworth.

"Did you see this?"

Em took the paper and read it. She tossed it back to Maeko then closed her eyes and leaned her head back on the seat. "Why must things always get worse?"

•

A short time later, they drew up along a familiar street. The coach stopped a few houses down from Maeko's mother's house. Maeko had run away as a child, believing her mother didn't want her anymore. Only recently, she had discovered that Tomoe's decision to send her to an orphanage wasn't because she didn't want her. Tomoe hadn't believed she could protect Maeko from the men who had cut up her face in the brothel, leaving her with scars and medical bills that forced her into debt with a mysterious benefactor. That benefactor required her to serve as a laundress while providing illegal medical care and safe haven for injured Pirates dodging the law—a practice she continued even now.

Knowing her mother never really wanted her gone wasn't enough by itself to restore the feeling of family between them, not yet, but someday perhaps, when the sting of old wounds faded.

"I see you recognize the place. Amos tracked your good friend Asher to that house last night. Place belongs to a Japanese woman by the name of Tomoe Ishida. Maybe you know her." The meaningful look Em gave her then said she at least suspected the connection. "She's a laundress with a very interesting past and some rather unusual connections considering her trade."

Maeko said nothing.

"I can drop you here and come back this evening if you want to visit, but don't even think about skipping out on your side of our agreement. Amos is hiding out nearby keeping an eye on the place for me. If you pull anything, it could mean trouble for Ms. Ishida."

"I told you I would help you," Maeko hissed. "Threatening my family isn't necessary."

Em smirked. "So she is your mum. I bet there's a fascinating story behind that."

Maeko glared at her.

"You've skipped out on me before, Rat. I guess I find it a little hard to trust you."

"I think I had good reason." Maeko scanned the street then opened the door. When her feet touched the ground, she turned back to Em. The soaking rain falling cold on her head and shoulders didn't cool her blazing temper. "I don't know what happened to you to make you this way, but someday you'll die alone and no one will care."

She slammed the coach door and trudged through the wet street, making her way to her mother's door. The cold rain felt good on her sore back and neck. Good enough that she stood outside the door for a minute and let it run down under the collar of the jacket Em had given her before she knocked.

Lottie, the buxom blond who shared the house with Tomoe, answered and ushered her into the cramped structure, lit sparingly by a few candles around the main room.

"Maeko-chan." Tomoe stood up from a chair and set aside the trousers she'd been stitching. She folded her hands in front of her and bowed. The scars on her face didn't detract from the serene Asian elegance that had made her so popular in the brothel. "Ogenki deska?"

"Okaasan." Maeko offered a small bow in return. A deep rift remained between them, the bridge not burned perhaps, but certainly rickety. "Genki desu."

Before Maeko could say more, the blanket that had been hung to separate the back section of the house when Tomoe was caring for Captain Garrett's gunshot wound shifted and Ash came around. He saw her and a tenuous smile touched his lips.

"I was worried about you. Are you all right?"

The sight of him brought that last kiss with Chaff sweeping to the forefront of her thoughts, sending blood rushing to her cheeks. She shifted her feet, struggling to push the memory away and meet his eyes. She hoped the poor lighting would hide her flush. "I just told Mum I was."

"I don't speak Japanese," he answered with a grin.

Her cheeks flushed hotter. "Sorry."

"You do not look all right." Tomoe strode over to her, her gaze on Maeko's neck where the bruising reached around the side.

"It's nothing you can help with. Just bruises. It'll heal." Maeko raised a hand to ward her off. "Why are you still helping Pirates? Mr. Folesworth paid your debt."

"It is what I do." Tomoe's lips pressed into a fine line, her eyes still on the bruising.

Ash frowned. "What happened?"

There would be no more talk of the debt if the hard look in her mother's eyes were any indication. Maeko turned to Ash. "I had a run in with a very strong, very unfriendly bloke." She fended off Tomoe's second attempt to take a closer look with one hand, doing her best to hide the pain all that movement caused, and stepped further into the room, close enough to Ash to see the red rimming his eyes and the shadows under them. "I heard they arrested your dad."

He clenched his teeth and looked away. "They did. He didn't want to believe what you told me. Said he needed to find out for himself, but he sent me, Sam, and Mum off with the airship just in case. They took him in for questioning and never let him leave."

Someone else stepped around the curtain then, a man with unkempt raven black hair and eyes almost as dark. He had sharp features that put her in mind of a wolf and a shifty gaze that put her on her guard. Although he was slight of build and not that much taller than Tomoe, something about his presence, a certain air of threat, made him intimidating. He gave her quick measuring look, which she returned with equal scorn.

His lip curled in a sneer under his black moustache. "Who's the rat?"

Tomoe's eyes flashed. "This young lady is my daughter, Maeko, Drake-san, and you would do well to remember whose house you are in."

Maeko couldn't help but smile at her mother's frosty tone. Maybe that bridge was a little stronger than she thought.

"I suppose it is your house now. My apologies." The sneer went away, but those dark eyes measured her without kindness. He came forward and offered Maeko his hand. He wore black leather gloves. "Drake please, not Mr. Drake or Drake-san."

He looked rather like a drake to her and his comment about the house suggested he was connected somehow to the man who'd held her mum in servitude for so long. She kept her hands at her sides. "You're a Pirate?"

His eyes narrowed a touch. He retracted his hand. "Yes. And an inventor."

He pulled the glove off the hand he had offered her and she took a step back. The hand was metal, fully articulated and far more refined than the one that had almost crushed her neck, but it whispered of the same workmanship and style.

"You look like you've seen a ghost," he murmured, his dark gaze searching her face.

"You've made something like this before."

He started to pull the glove back on. "Yes. For a rather unpleasant bloke. He never did pay me for the work, but I needed a willing subject with a missing arm to test the design. I couldn't be overly choosy. I presume by your reaction that you've met him."

Was that as far as the association went? "I have and I can assure you he won't be coming around to pay that debt off."

Drake shrugged. He gave her another measuring look and a crooked smile turned up one corner of his mouth. His initial assessment appeared to be changing. "It wasn't my best work. As you can see, I've made extensive improvements." He smoothed the glove over the false hand then met her eyes. "You're the one who told Garrett's boy—"

"I'm right here," Ash snapped.

"Yes," Drake snapped back. He didn't look away from her. "You say Lucian Folesworth is dead?"

She nodded, clenching her teeth against the painful resistance in her neck. All this activity was catching up with her too soon.

His gaze turned inward. "I don't see why they would kill the mind behind the company. Where do they expect to get new designs?"

"Why? Are you hoping to apply for the position?"

"I'm starting to like you. You've a sharp tongue, but a clever mind." Drake grinned. "No, I'm trying to understand the motivation of my enemies."

Ash was watching them with a look of growing irritation. He began to tap one foot. For the moment, he would have to be patient. She wasn't going to give Drake any easy answers until she understood his position better and there was only one way to figure that out.

"What makes you so sure they're your enemies?"

"Thaddeus Folesworth and Joel Jacard are Literati supporters to their core. If you're right, and I'm willing to accept that you might be, then whatever they're up to can't be good for the Pirates."

If he was willing to give her that much credit, then perhaps she could return the favor. "I've been through Lucian's files. There are hundreds of sketches for items not in production. Plenty of ideas to keep Clockwork Enterprises developing new products for years and more than a few are for weapons and false appendages similar to yours." *And Macak's.* She didn't think it safe to mention the cat to him, not yet.

Drake's false hand clenched into a fist and she shifted away. He didn't seem to notice. "Weapon designs," he muttered. "Why didn't he say...?" He trailed off and, after a minute, his hand relaxed. "I do hope you'll be joining us. You've got a useful head on your shoulders for a girl."

"I'm not a Pirate."

"Better to be a street rat?"

She almost said it was safer, but then that didn't ring true anymore. Pirate or not, events had pushed her to their side of the conflict. She turned to Ash. "Why are you still here?"

Drake took that as an end to the conversation and vanished behind the curtain muttering to himself about weapons and people keeping secrets. Maeko shuddered. She didn't like something about him. Something rang false about his renegade Pirate inventor act. At least he seemed to be on their side and, like it or not, it was *their side* now. How had she gotten involved in this bollocks?

Macak trotted out from a dark corner of her mind and she smirked at the image.

Oh yes, you.

A cat with a remarkable leg hiding behind the same ashbin she happened to hide behind to escape the Lits. Fate worked in the strangest ways. If only she had left him to his lot instead of taking it upon herself to keep him safe, but then, she couldn't regret it.

"With my Dad locked up, I thought I should stay behind to help organize things." Ash answered in a hushed voice, scowling at the curtain as he moved closer to her.

"Why? What can you do?"

He turned his scowl on her then. "Why are *you* here? Shouldn't you be hiding out somewhere safe?"

She stared at the curtain, trying to decide how she felt about the man now hidden behind it. "I'm here to help the people I care about." How was she going to do that exactly? Now that she thought about it, what could she do?

"So am I," he countered. "So, does that mean..."

She caught the hope in his tone and glanced at him. "Don't be daft. You know I care about you."

He smiled then. Such a charming smile. She could feel Chaff's lips against hers, his hand on her hip, pulling her against him. She looked away, forcing her thoughts back to the current situation. Now that she thought about it, she'd always been working at odds with the Lits. With her mother and Ash allied with the Pirates, she really couldn't claim neutrality anymore. Perhaps it was time to stop denying it and dive into the fray.

"I still have a key to Lucian's flat," she said to no one in particular.

The curtain swept aside, confirming her suspicion that Drake was listening to them. The inventor's eyes gleamed like black diamonds. He smiled a wicked smile that made her very happy he didn't count her an enemy. Ash gave her a horrified look and Tomoe pressed her lips together in disapproval. Drake came forward and held his hand out to Maeko again. This time she took it. The metal hand closed on hers, the grip far gentler than she'd expected.

"Welcome aboard, Maeko."

CHAPTER SEVENTEEN

I can't go after Lucian's drawings tonight," Maeko objected.

Tomoe and Ash were watching them, both still wearing expressions of deepest displeasure. Chaff wore a similar expression in her head. The tongue-lashing she would get from him if he found out what she was doing would probably hurt for years.

Ash stepped closer to her. "Why does she have to go at all?"

Drake gave a long-suffering sigh and turned an impatient gaze on Ash. "Because she has the key, she knows the building, she knows where the drawings are, and she's versed in the fine art of stealth. Tell me which of those things you can claim?"

Ash set his jaw and glared back in defiant silence, unable to argue with any of those points.

Drake turned his gaze back to her. "We can't hide out here much longer. With escalating violence on the streets, it's only a matter of time before some injured Pirate is followed here. We need to move to a safer place soon. Why can't you do it tonight?"

"I have other..." She trailed off, reconsidering the situation. Now that she thought about it, the Airship Tower might be the best place to draw out Em's shooter if he really was working for Thaddeus. Of course, she'd want to get the drawings out of the building first. If she could find a way to get those to Drake before calling attention to herself then she could put all her risk into one night and be done with it. Ash was staring at her, concern drawing his brows together. There was no way to make everyone happy, but if she could help the cause her mum had taken up at the same time she helped Em's investigations, didn't it make sense to do so?

"Maybe I can go tonight, but I'll need help. I can't come back here with the drawings right away. I've got other business to attend to. If Ash could meet me somewhere behind the building, I can pass the drawings off to him and he can bring them back here while I see to my other obligations."

The tension coming from Ash lifted a little now that he was part of the plan, but Drake raised an eyebrow in question. "Other obligations? That's mysterious. I thought we were working together now."

"On this we are, but I have prior commitments. If you want those drawings, you'll have to accept that."

There was the heart of it. He wanted the drawings badly and it showed. He nodded, though his lip curled as if he'd swallowed something he didn't like the taste of. Her secrecy didn't sit well with him. He turned to Ash. "You'll need to send word to your mum. This little caper will draw a lot of unwanted attention. Staying here will put Tomoe in danger. Tell Julia to pick us up out back tomorrow night."

Ash nodded, solemn. He took his duties seriously. It was cute. Maeko caught herself smiling fondly at him and looked away, but not before he caught the expression and beamed back at her.

Drake shook his head and rubbed at the bridge of his nose with the thumb and forefinger of his normal hand, the small sneer of distaste still twisting his lip.

Whatever he had against Ash, he needed to set it

aside if they were going to work on this together. Maeko gave him a hard look.

He caught her meaning and schooled his expression to neutrality.

She bobbed her head in a small nod of appreciation. "We need to figure out a time and a drop point. Ash needs to be in position before I'm out of the Tower. As long as he stays hidden until I'm clear of the building, I should be able to draw off any unwanted attention."

Ash started to protest and Drake threw up a hand to silence him. He gave her a shrewd look. "You intended to get their attention anyway, didn't you? Why? What are you trying to accomplish?"

Ash gave her a startled look and Tomoe began to stab her needle through the trousers she'd gone back to mending as if they needed killing.

Maeko held Drake's gaze and said nothing.

"Mae?" Ash prompted.

She ignored him, staring into the black eyes in front of her.

"You're right, it isn't my business," Drake conceded.

Ash sputtered and she turned on him. "You need to do this without worrying about what I'm doing. Can you do that? If not, I'll have to find another way to get the drawings back here."

He clenched his jaw and stared at her. Resistance backlit his beautiful eyes. "Mae, you know I can't help worrying about you."

"Then we'll find someone else," Drake stated, his tone frosty. "I can't risk being recognized by the Lits. Perhaps Tomoe or Lottie?"

"No!" Ash slapped a hand down on the table next to him. "I'll do it."

"Are you sure?" She held his gaze.

"I am."

•

When Em's coach appeared early that evening in the still-driving rain, Maeko slipped out of the house, not giving Ash time to put words to the worry in his expression. She climbed into the coach and explained the plan.

"You're helping the Pirates now?"

"It's better than helping Lits."

Em grimaced. "That's debatable, but we'll do it so long as you're quick. The Tower is a good place to try waving the bait. I'll drop you a few blocks out and you can take care of your burglary. I'll park the coach a block down from the teahouse and wait for you. We'll be watching the Tower. Once you're outside, head our direction. Don't get into trouble inside. If you do, you're on your own."

Maeko swallowed a lump of fear. What would Thaddeus do to her if he found her there? She hated to think about it. "That's where I need another favor from you. I need you to drop me at the lurk. Chaff and I will catch a hansom to the Tower. That way you can show up separately and avoid the risk of someone seeing me get out of your coach near the building."

"You're taking the kidsman with you?" Her expression and tone conveyed mounds of disapproval.

Maeko ignored it, though she was still uneasy about involving Chaff. He would be happier if he could keep an eye on her and she would be safer with someone watching her back. "He and I work well together."

"What else do you do well together?" Em's tone was too suggestive.

"Ha ha," Maeko returned with a sour glare, though she couldn't stop the slight flush when her mind wandered to other ways in which they might fit well together. She shifted her shoulders, hoping pain would provide adequate distraction.

•

"This is a bad idea, Pigeon."

"Please, Chaff."

"You're injured." He paced the room, resistance in the snap of his strides. Macak paced with him, a fuzzy shadow, making it hard not to giggle from where she watched seated on his cot.

"That's why I need you with me. I know the building. I have the key even. I just need someone who can help me out if I get in a fix. I'm not that agile right now."

He stopped and stared at her. "All the more reason to let it go."

"It's a straightforward burglary. We have more inside information and easier access to the building than we normally would. And I'm going, with or without you."

"Not if I throw you over my shoulder and take you to Whitechapel."

The flash of his eyes told her he would do it.

"Blast it, Chaff," she popped to her feet, a flare of pain making her regret her haste, though she refused to acknowledge it. "I didn't have to ask for help. I came here because I trust you more than anyone. I came here because—"

Whatever she'd been about to say disappeared when he stepped into her, his lips claiming hers in a hard kiss. She wanted to be angry with him for interrupting, but her body had already forgiven the infraction. She pressed against him, meeting the demand in his kiss with equal intensity, all of her frustration with him, her confusion with Ash, and her fear poured into that kiss. His hands slid down to her waist, working under her shirt to press warm against skin that sparked to life under his touch, awakening a flood of desire that threatened to make her forget the trials she faced outside that room.

His hands started to move up under her shirt, sliding over her skin. She knew she should stop him, but she didn't want to. She wanted to forget the pain and let the fear go. His hands stopped on their own and he slid them back down, settling them at her waist and pushing her back. Warm blue eyes gazed down at her.

"You have no idea how much I want to keep going."

She bit her lip, not trusting herself to respond, but she suspected she had more idea than he realized.

"If we're going to do this thing and get you to Whitechapel where you can finish healing, we'd better get moving. I'll send our stuff over there with one of my boys."

Finish healing, in your care...

All she could do was nod. Her voice got stuck behind the shame of what she'd almost done, leaving everyone hanging to hide away in the comfort of his embrace, and for the guilt of knowing she hadn't told him everything. He didn't know she was acting as bait to help Em find the commissioners killer. He wouldn't let her go if he did.

"What about the cat?" He asked, not looking at her now.

Was that because he didn't want her to see him wanting her or was there something else? Did he suspect she was hiding things?

"We take him with us?"

"Here I hoped you were falling for my charms. Now I know you've just gone barmy." He glanced her direction, still not quite looking at her.

Was she falling for him? Was she merely desperate for the comfort of someone's embrace? Would Ash have worked as well in his place? Why were relationships so bloody confusing?

"Macak's got better hearing than either of us. He's a good early warning."

Chaff put a hand to his forehead, closing his eyes and shaking his head once. Then he looked at her. His expression tightened and he looked away again. Why did that avoidance make her chest hurt so?

"All right, Pigeon, we do it your way."

The night was cold. Rain fell in a steady patter now, not quite as heavy as before. As miserable as the weather was, it did drown out some of the stench of the city. The Tower lobby glowed with subdued nighttime lighting in the dark, warm and inviting. For a short time, she had been welcome beyond those fancy doors. No longer. She shivered and considered trying to slip in through the front. Perhaps they wouldn't stop her. If Thaddeus hadn't declared her missing, maybe they wouldn't be on the watch for her. The young desk attendant was there. He seemed to like her.

No. She had to remember that she wasn't dressed like a young lady anymore. Her presence was sure to draw attention in these inappropriate togs. Even if they did let her go in the way she was dressed, she'd never get Chaff and Macak past them and the job would be over before it began.

Cold and wet, she led the way around to the back of the building, to the door she'd left through the night Lucian died. She knew how the latch worked now. It wouldn't be so hard to pick. She drew out the lock pick tools and went to work on it.

Chaff huddled next to her, Macak watching with bright-eyed interest from the cradle of his arms. Her back and neck ached with all the activity, reminding her of the warmth and care he'd given her over the last few days. She envied the cat his place in those arms.

The lock released. She tucked the picks away and nudged the door open. When they were inside, she locked it behind her and crept up along the wall of the conference room, staying in the deepest shadows. Macak, now on the ground, trotted a few strides ahead of them, his ears perked, also staying in the shadows. The door to the lobby opened and they all froze, crouching against the wall next to a table. Her heartbeat sped up.

A guard entered and started across the room toward the door. He glanced around once, but didn't see them. Having come from the bright lobby, his eyes wouldn't be adjusted to the dim room yet. She met Chaff's eyes as he passed them. Chaff nodded and they crept fast along the wall once the guard was far enough past not to catch their movement on his periphery. Better not to give him time to look around after his eyes adjusted and one less guard in the lobby would be to their advantage if they moved fast enough.

The door to the lobby stood cracked and she peered in. Two guards were watching the front doors. A third leaned on the front desk, having a chinwag with the desk attendant. Holding her breath, she snatched up Macak, slipped through the door and scurried to the staircase. Once out of sight, she pressed back against the wall and waited for Chaff. She stopped holding her breath and set Macak down when he joined them, giving him a game grin as though she weren't terrified. As though this were any other job.

He reached out and gave her hand a squeeze, seeing through her ruse. "I've got your back," he murmured.

She gave up the grin and continued up the stairs as fast as she dared, freezing and listening at every little sound, pausing to listen any time Macak hesitated.

At the top, she crossed to the door and crouched with her ear to the edge, listening. Chaff did the same at the other edge of the door. Nothing. She counted to sixty twice, reached for the door handle, waiting for his nod before she tested the door. Locked. She used the key and pushed the door open a crack. Macak slipped inside. The delicious aromas of that evening's supper wafted out along with the faint scent of pipe smoke. Her stomach grumbled. She counted to sixty again, listening and hoping Macak wouldn't draw attention.

The only sound was the ticking of the standing clock in the dining room. She and Chaff slipped inside and shut the door. The memory of the woman and child lying dead on the floor the first time they'd entered this flat rushed to the forefront of her mind.

It could be me there next. Worse, it could be Chaff and it would be my fault for dragging him into this. She shuddered. *Focus.*

She skirted well around that part of the floor, Chaff shadowing her every move, and crept down the hallway to Lucian's study. Macak was already there, sitting outside and cleaning one paw as if to say they were terribly slow. There she paused and put her ear to the door, listening for another sixty seconds even though no telltale light shone under. The soft click when she opened the door was like a thunderclap to her strung out nerves.

Chaff slipped inside with her and positioned himself at the door, keeping it cracked so he could watch down the hall. Her heart thrummed in her ears, giving her a rhythm to focus on as she slid open the cabinet and began to pull files out, piling the sketches together in one folder. When she finished, she had a thick stack of pages crammed into the folder. Someone had emptied a few of the folders already, but she didn't dare take time to look around and see if those drawings were still in the room. She handed the fat folder to Chaff who tucked it under his coat. They left the study with Macak leading the way.

Now all that remained was to get out again and send Chaff to deliver the sketches to Ash. Then she could focus on her role as bait for a killer, the thought of which made her skin crawl.

Halfway down the hall, Macak froze. They followed his lead and she heard someone moving out in the kitchen. She caught Chaff's eyes and gestured to the cat. He gave a tight smile and nodded. A light flickered on, spreading a blanket of illumination out through the kitchen doorway. They ducked back down the hall to stay well out of its reach.

Please don't come down here.

After a short time, the light went out and she heard footsteps retreating down the other hall. She let out her breath and hurried out of the flat. When the locked clicked home again, she stood and took a few deep breaths, Chaff watching her with narrowed eyes.

He knows I'm up to something else. She forced her breathing to slow. *Calm and silent.* Haste and panic led to foolish mistakes.

Her heartbeat slowed. The fear tickling up the back of her spine faded. Pain from her injuries swelled in the calm. For the moment, she would have to ignore that. With a firm nod, she began to descend the stairs. As they passed the seventh floor landing, Macak stopped in their path again. They froze and heard footsteps coming up. There was nowhere to hide here, so they pressed back against the inside corner. Chaff crouched down and she shifted to the side so the approaching person would see her first.

A guard came around the corner. His eyes locked on Maeko, going wide when Chaff kicked out, knocking his feet out from under him. He tumbled down the rest of that flight. He was still breathing when they ran past, his eyes closed as if in sleep. She sprinted down, snatching up Macak on her way. No one in the lobby would have heard the fall, but someone on the near floors might have. Best to move on before someone investigated. She hoped someone had heard and would come to the guard's aid. She didn't want to hurt him. He was only doing his job. The up side of running into him on the stairs was that there wouldn't be more than three guards in the lobby again.

She swallowed the coppery taste of fear. This wasn't the usual break-in job. Usually the greatest threat was being arrested, not something she was too keen on, but better than some options. This time, if she were caught, there was a fair chance the consequences would be far more severe. If Thaddeus wanted her dead before, this would only strengthen his resolve to see it done.

At the last turn of the stairs, they pressed against the corner again and she peeked around. The one guard still stood chatting up the desk attendant, but now another had joined them. They apparently took their job quite seriously. The third stood scowling at the other two, perhaps sharing her sentiment, but paying no more attention to the rest of the area in the process.

She stuck tight to the back wall and snuck out through the door into the conference room. It was hard not to sprint for the back door, but experience told her to expect the worst when victory was closest, and she needed to wait for Chaff. The end of a job was always when one stumbled upon an unexpected extra guard or someone who couldn't sleep wandering the halls of a quiet house.

Chaff slipped in, clicking the door shut and giving her a quick nod. She stayed tight to the darkest side of the room and moved across to the rear door.

Only a few feet from her target she spotted another lurker in the room. The rat creeping across the room spotted her at the same moment and froze, whiskers twitching; his black eyes tiny beads in the dark. Macak squirmed in her arms. She held the cat snug and grinned at the rat.

"Neighborhood's going to the dogs, isn't it?" she whispered.

The rat squeaked and scampered off in the other direction and Chaff muffled a laugh in his hand, shaking his head at her though a smile lit his eyes.

They reached the back door and she took a deep breath. It only opened out so she had to take a leap of faith. She pushed it open and stepped out. There was no one around that she could see. The rain had picked up again, a full on downpour. She peered up and down the street. Chaff stepped out with her.

Please be ready Ash.

When the rest of her sweep didn't bring anyone to her attention, she moved to the corner, finding the deepest shadows to stop in.

"Ash should be two blocks that way at the corner. Take the folder to him and meet me back at the lurk in an hour. We'll head to Whitechapel from there." *I hope.* "Don't let the sketches get wet."

"Blast it, Pigeon," Chaff grabbed her arm. "Where are you going?"

"Don't worry about it. If you don't make a scene and draw attention, I'll be fine. I'll see you later. Ganbatte." She gave his hand a stern look. When he reluctantly let go, she walked away, not giving him time to argue more. His soft "ganbatte" followed her and she hugged Macak a little closer.

Now for the tricky part. If the man they were looking for was somewhere around or in the building, she needed to get his attention, but she didn't want to be too obvious about it. It seemed unlikely that he would shoot her in the open right outside the Tower, though the mere possibility made her skin prickle. There weren't many people out this late in such miserable weather, but Thaddeus couldn't want another incident so close to home.

To keep attention away from Chaff on his way to meet Ash, she moved back around the opposite side of the building and crossed the street before walking down the block in front of the Tower. She made a show of trying to stick to the deeper shadows, enough so to draw the suspicion of anyone who might be watching for trouble.

She was less than a block from Em's coach before she actually saw it through the still increasing downpour. It was starting to feel like walking through a waterfall. A waterfall in flood no less. Macak was trying to crawl inside her clothing to escape the wet and she could only get so annoyed with him. This was rubbish. How would anyone even spot her in this? Maybe Em would have to call it off and try another night. Besides, she was getting cold enough now that she had started to shiver and that wasn't helping her pain in the least. She stopped trying to keep to deeper shadows and made a direct line to the waiting coach.

The coach driver sat hunkered down, his hat pulled low on his forehead.

Poor chap must hate his job on nights like this.

She walked up and grabbed the door, yanking it open. Macak twisted in her arms, digging in his claws and scrabbling free of her grasp as she ducked into the dark interior to get out of the rain. He sprinted back out into the downpour and she began to turn to go after him when someone grabbed her wrists, yanking them up behind her and flipping her around face down on the narrow floor of the coach.

Pain streaked through Maeko's back and neck with the force of a lightning bolt, stealing her breath away. Someone else stepped up into the coach behind her and shut the door. The new arrival pounded on the roof and it began to move. She couldn't get her head around far enough to see either of them.

The man holding her wrists, at least she assumed it was a man given the size of his hands and his strength, lifted her and she twisted around, kicking out so her foot caught the second man across the jaw. The maneuver sent a flare of pain through her back that stole her breath away again. One hand let go of her wrists and something struck the back of her head. The interior of the coach spun around her and she sank to her knees, dazed. All she could do for several agonizing seconds was try to catch her breath and not be sick.

A soft click drew her attention to the man now sitting on the seat she was facing. He wore a bowler cap low on his head. It shadowed his features. He held a gun in one hand rested across his lap, the hammer cocked. He touched a finger to his lips and she flinched when he spit blood on the seat in front of her face.

"Not much of a lady, kicking your host like that before we've even said hello." He had a soft voice, a familiar voice that made her skin crawl.

"Joel Jacard?" Her voice cracked, betraying the swell of terror that made her throbbing head spin faster.

He raised his head enough that she could see his face and smiled. He looked thinner for his brief stay in the jail, but no saner.

Wearing a smug grin, he took his hand away from the gun to draw a cigarette out of his pocket and struck a lucifer. After lighting the cigarette, he ground out the match on the seat, leaving a scorch mark there next to the wet spot of blood.

"I've been keen to see you again, Rat. I believe I owe you something for shooting me. My arm still doesn't work right, which is why I had to have Bennett join our little liaison." He nodded to the man behind her. "He's quite practiced in the handling of little problems."

Her wrists ached, still twisted back in the other man's tight grip, and the position set her back on fire. "Little problems like Commissioner Henderson?"

Joel's expression was cold and unyielding, but she wasn't going to let him trick her. They were responsible for the commissioner's death. She was certain of it. She'd drawn out the killer as planned. Too bad the blasted detective wasn't holding up her end of the deal. But Em wouldn't have abandoned her like this, not if she had a choice, and that didn't help settle her nerves.

She licked her lips and asked, "Where's Em?"

"I imagine she's a bit preoccupied right about now." Joel chuckled. "I think you have enough troubles of your own to worry about, don't you?" He sucked on the cigarette and exhaled nauseating stale smoke into her face. "What were you doing in the Tower?"

She fought to gather her thoughts through the haze of pain from her various injuries. The blow to the head hadn't helped with clarity, nor did the building terror making her insides into a quivering mess. Did they know about Chaff or Ash? "You saw me go inside?"

"We saw you arrive with the other rat a bit before the detective pulled in down the street. I figured you were all up to something. Mr. Folesworth has enough to deal with right now, so I thought it would be most practical to wait until you came out to the coach where we could have a little private meeting to work out our differences." He took another draw on the cigarette and blew smoke in her face again.

She coughed and turned away. "How delightful."

"Back to my question. What were you doing in the Tower?"

One wheel hit a pothole, jarring the coach and sending a spike of pain through the tender spot on her head where the other man had struck her. She ground her teeth and fought to focus. Not that it mattered now. There wasn't much chance of escaping them in the tight confines of the coach. She just had to keep her wits long enough to get wherever they were going and reassess the situation. "We were trying to lure out the man who shot the commissioner."

Joel glanced at the man behind her, mock severity in his tone. "Did you kill Commissioner Henderson." The man behind her remained ominously silent. Joel shrugged. "I didn't think so. You're barking up the wrong tree, Rat."

"I am not," she grumbled. One of them was wearing heavy cologne that made her unbalanced stomach clench. She swallowed hard to fight the urge to retch.

"This is how we ended up enemies, Rat. You can't keep your nose out of other people's business."

Pain made it hard to breathe, hard to focus. Joel's mocking tone crushed her, bringing the sting of hopeless tears to her eyes. They both knew he had won. Without Em, there was no one who would know to come to her aid and she couldn't fight them like this. She ground her teeth, fighting back the threatening tears. She wouldn't give him the satisfaction of seeing her cry. There was still hope. There had to be.

"What do you expect me to say? We both know you aren't going to let me go."

His smile faded. "No, I'm not. I wouldn't get any satisfaction out of that. However, I can't have your body showing up near the Tower and disrupting poor Lucian in his time of mourning so we have a few more minutes to discuss where you've been spreading your lies about Mr. Folesworth's situation before we wrap up our little meeting. Have you told anyone other than your little detective friend?"

They weren't lies. They couldn't be. Lucian was dead. She was certain of it, wasn't she? What if she was wrong? "Go to hell."

Bennett twisted her arms back hard and she cried out. Joel released the hammer on his gun and set it on the far side of the seat, well out of her reach. He leaned forward. The coach rolled to a stop. Part of her wanted to curl up in a quivering ball and beg for her life, but she couldn't disgrace herself that way, not in front of him. It wouldn't do any good beyond giving him a chuckle anyway.

End of the road. She hoped Macak found safety. He was a victim in all of this chaos.

"I guess we're out of time, but when it comes down to it, I don't really care what lies you told and who you told them to." He leaned down, putting his face in front of her. "After what you put me through, I only regret that I don't have time to stick around and watch you die."

His breath smelled like smoke and rotten fish. Her stomach heaved and she couldn't stop the rush of bile this time. Joel hopped sideways on the seat, avoiding the spray of vomit with all but the very edge of his trouser leg. He sneered and nodded to the man behind her who began to bind her wrists with an abrasive rope. She twisted, terror giving her strength. Both men grabbed her and threw her face down on the floor again. Joel pressed a foot down between her shoulder blades, his boot heel digging into bruised muscles across her back. He picked up the gun. She squeezed her eyes shut, waiting for the shot. Something struck her head and darkness sucked her down.

Cold snapped her to awareness again with a gasp. Foul tasting water filled her mouth. Water surrounded her. She was sinking, her hands bound behind her back. She choked. Coherent thought swept away on the wave of panic and terror searing through her. She swallowed more water. Her hands twisted against the coarse rope, grinding away skin. She kicked hard, slowing her descent, but gaining no upward momentum. Her lungs strained, aching for air. Her eyes darted around, finding nothing but darkness. So dark and alone and cold.

I'm not wrong.

Her eyes started to sting. Was that tears or just the filthy black water?

Why couldn't they have just shot me?

The thought brought a manic giddiness with it and she almost laughed before self-preservation kicked in and stopped her from drawing more water into her lungs. She kicked her feet again, weaker this time. Black threatened at the edges of her vision. Her body trembled with the effort of not breathing in. She tried to kick again. The effort was too much.

I'm sorry Chaff.

There was no doubt now that tears were at least part of what made her eyes sting. She began to sink again. Her lungs ached. Her head pounded. The water was cold, numbing. She squeezed her eyes shut against the sting and the black crept in, closing around her.

CHAPTER TWENTY

Maeko's stomach heaved and she rolled onto her side. She threw up foul water and the little bit of food that remained in her gut. Someone's arms wrapped around her, pulling her away from the vomit and guiding her up to her hands and knees. A fit of coughing sent shooting pain through her back and neck. Her limbs shook so hard she couldn't hold herself up so she sagged into the arms that held her.

"Give me your jacket."

Chaff? *How*? Everything was so cold. Shaking took all her energy away from simple tasks like speaking.

A jacket appeared from somewhere. Someone yanked her sopping jacket off and Chaff wrapped the dry jacket around her.

So cold. So tired. She closed her eyes.

"Pigeon, talk to me."

She wanted to. It was much too hard though. Her lips felt numb. Her thoughts were sluggish and broken. She needed to rest. He shook her. Desperate to avoid more rough handling, she made her eyes obey, opening them for a second. They slid closed a second later, not giving her enough time to make sense of her surroundings.

"We need to get her dry and warm."

Em?

She tried to open her eyes again. This time they refused to obey. Someone lifted her, someone as wet and cold as she was. She tried to push away from the wet body, wanting to escape that extra chill, but the arms held her tight. She gave up, much too weak and exhausted to fight. All she wanted was a little rest.

•

The shivering wouldn't stop. It hurt in her bruised muscles and it sapped her energy. It also kept her from sleep, but she could do nothing to control it.

"This is your fault." Chaff sounded angry.

"She agreed to the plan," Em snapped. "She knew the risks."

"I doubt she expected this."

Em was silent a moment. When she spoke again, she sounded almost as tired as Maeko felt. "Neither did I."

Her eyelids felt heavy. For that matter, her whole body felt like a weight of bricks lay on top of it. She was still so cold. With great effort, she managed to open her eyes. The first thing she noticed was old green wallpaper peeling off the opposite wall. The room smelled of cheap perfume, a ghastly stench that made her empty stomach cramp. Em stood in one corner glaring at someone outside Maeko's line of sight. The detective had a bloody scrape on one cheek, a spectacular black eye swelled nearly shut and a thick blood-soaked bandage wrapped around one forearm.

"You're not dead." Maeko's voice came out hoarse and slurred. The effort made her cough.

Em looked at her and shook her head. "Less so than you at least."

The door opened and Diggs leaned in with a heavy blanket in hand. Chaff stepped out from the corner of the room Em had been glaring into and took it. He gave

Em a long hard look. The detective sneered and stormed from the room after Diggs, slamming the door behind them. The coughing eased and Maeko closed her eyes for a moment, trying to regain her breath. Her head throbbed. Chaff added the new blanket to the several already weighing her down then touched her cheek.

She opened her eyes again. His hair was wet. He wore a tortured expression as if someone dear had died and he were trying to hold back the sorrow. Trying to be strong like he always was. He held a cup out in one hand. The hand shook a little. She tried to shift up on her elbow to take it. The strength simply wasn't there. She gave up, a sigh of weariness whispering between her lips. Chaff set the cup down and helped her up, sitting next to her so she could lean on him.

"Drink this." He held it to her lips, tipping it up a touch.

She took a small sip. It was hot and a little sweet. It burned going down. She started to cough and he moved the cup away until the coughing passed again. He brought it back to her lips and she managed to swallow without coughing this time. After several drinks, she put a hand up and pushed the cup weakly away. He relented, taking a swallow himself before setting it aside. The shivering let up a little.

"How?" It was as much talking as she had energy for yet. She figured it would translate well enough.

"I know you, Pigeon. I knew you'd find trouble the minute you left me. I passed off the package to your boy and struck out after you. I came on the detective in time to save her being shot, or shot in a fatal way anyhow. We were making our escape from that sticky situation when that cat—"

"Macak," she corrected.

There was a hint of smile in his voice when he continued. "Macak came sprinting out of the rain at us.

We were just lucky to catch sight of the coach before it got too far and tail it to the river."

"You dove in after me," she murmured, knowing it was true without needing his confirmation.

"What else was I going to do?"

She managed a fleeting smile. "Did they see you?"

"No. I don't believe so."

"Good. Then they'll think I'm dead."

He put his arms around her and squeezed her tight. She didn't mind the pain it caused in her back. Not at all.

He kissed her head. "You almost were."

The shivering still shook her, continuing to sap her strength. She curled against him, closing her eyes. He reached out and pulled the blankets in around her. She listened to his heartbeat, letting the steady rhythm lull her until a more violent bout of shivering took hold and jarred her back to miserable awareness. Tears of frustration slipped out, hot on her icy skin.

Chaff shifted her, encouraging her to lie down again. She squeezed her eyes shut and curled under the blankets, trying to get warm. Moments later, he slipped into the covers behind her. He wrapped his arms around her and pulled her in against him. It wasn't until then that she realized she wasn't dressed. Someone had stripped away her sopping clothes before putting her in the bed. Chaff had taken off everything but his drawers. The pain in her bruises and the lack of appropriate clothes became unimportant, however, when weighed against the warmth of his bare skin against her icy back.

She felt him wrap himself around her, savoring his warmth. If only it could reach the cold at her core. He moved his lips next to her ear and whispered to her while he held her to him.

"Remember when we first met? You were trying to nick a meal from a vendor's cart and I told you that you were going about it all wrong. You told me to bugger

off. You said you didn't need help from a bloody street
rat."

She smiled tiredly. She had said exactly those things,
just that crudely. He'd laughed and told her she had a lot
of cheek for a bird and she'd stomped on his foot before
storming away. It was the turbulent start of what would
become a brilliant partnership.

He continued to speak, reminiscing on past
escapades, the ongoing monologue holding her at the
edge of sleep. Eventually, the shivering stopped and she
began to feel warm again. He stopped talking then and
the silence allowed her to sink the rest of the way into
sleep.

•

When she woke, Chaff was gone. Every muscle and joint
ached and her head throbbed. Tentative fingers found
the lump where one of the men had struck her before
dropping her into the river. She groaned and opened her
eyes to find a woman in a corset and bright skirt, drawn
up in front to reveal even brighter layers of petticoats,
sitting in a chair by the bed. Her face was painted and
she wore high boots and stockings. A dollymop if
Maeko ever saw one, which meant they'd taken refuge
in a brothel. That explained the cheap perfume and
other questionable smells in the air.

"Where am I?" Her voice came out stronger now, if
a bit raspy.

"Relax, sweetie. Yer safe enough. If ye come with
me, I'll 'elp ye clean the river smell away and we'll get
ye back with yer friends. Yer beau's already 'ad 'imself a
bath."

Maeko flushed at that and considered arguing that
Chaff wasn't her beau, but there didn't seem to be much
sense in it.

The woman helped Maeko up and into a robe, then guided her down a dark hall with wood floors worn soft and rippled by years of human traffic to a candlelit room with a tub. Hot water startled her to attention, burning through much of the grogginess and making her more aware of the pain in her head. The woman began to clean her hair, mindful of the tender spots.

While the woman murmured compliments about her pretty hair and fair skin, Maeko closed her eyes, submitting to the gentle ministrations.

A short time later, the woman helped her out of the tub and dried her. Her clothes lay folded on a chair, no longer wet and, surprisingly, they didn't stink of the river. Someone must have cleaned them. Weakness and lethargy still sapped at her and everything ached from her mid-back to the top of her head, but at least she could think now and her joints no longer hurt. With the woman's help, she got dressed then the woman led her back to the hallway and pointed down it.

"Yer friends are in the room at the end. There's a warm fire and some stew waitin' too."

Her mouth watered at the thought. "Thank you, Miss."

She walked down the hall, feeling a touch unsteady on her feet. A large room opened up at the end with a few worn couches and chairs set around a table before a blazing fire. The fire itself was the only light in the room, making shadows dance in the darker corners. The hearty smell of the stew wafted up from a pot sitting on the hearth and two emptied bowls sat piled on the table. Diggs reclined in a chair with his feet up on the table and Macak curled in his lap. Chaff, despite all the available seating, stood leaning on the mantle staring into the fire.

"It's the way she is," Diggs said and Maeko took a quick step back, sinking into the shadows of the hallway to listen. "She's always been this way. You're only brassed off because she no longer looks to you for guidance before she jumps into things."

"I'm upset because she's going to get herself killed," Chaff snapped.

Diggs let the show of temper wash over him. He was good at that. The former mudlark never got riled about anything that she had seen. "That could be true, but she's like a cat, the tighter you hold her, the more she'll pull away. You know that. You either have to accept her the way she is or let her go."

Chaff said nothing, but the hand by his side clenched into a fist. Maeko waited a minute longer to see if either would speak again, and to make it less obvious that she'd heard them. When no one said anything more, she walked into the room.

"Where's Em?"

Chaff turned and walked over to her, the hand that had been a fist seconds ago came up to touch her face. He slid his fingers under her chin, a pleasant heat rising in their wake, and tilted her head back to search her eyes. "How are you feeling?"

She returned his gaze and tried hard not to think of his lean body wrapped around her in the bed, warming her, his skin pressed against hers in places she'd never been touched by anyone other than her mother. The vivid memory forced its way in despite her efforts and she lowered her gaze, hoping the darkness of the room would hide her flush.

"Better. A little weak. A little hungry too."

He smiled. "Hungry we can fix."

Chaff sat her down on one of the worn settees and insisted on serving her. While he did so, the subject of her query entered the room.

"Good to see you up and around."

For a few seconds, Maeko wasn't sure how to

respond to that. It was an unusually cordial greeting for
Em. "I...thanks. I was worried they'd killed you when
you weren't in the coach."

"They gave it a fair try." Em replied. Chaff's eyes
flickered up to the detective and she added, "thanks to a
timely intervention from your beau, they failed."

Maeko felt her cheeks warming again. All eyes
were on her, waiting for her to deny the role they had
assigned Chaff in her life. She wasn't entirely sure that
was what she wanted from their relationship, but what
would be the point in having a row about it? It wasn't
their business besides. She and Chaff could work that
out later.

"I think I know who shot the commissioner." She
caught Chaff's victorious grin as he wandered back over
to stare into the fire. Perhaps she should have argued.
Too late now.

"Thinking it and knowing it are two different things,
but it's more than we had before all this bollucks," Em
grumbled, her gaze also following Chaff to the fire.
Her eyes flickered back to Maeko after a few seconds.
"Who's the suspect?"

"Creepy bloke by the name of Bennett," she couldn't
stop a shudder when she spoke the name. "He's working
with Joel and Thaddeus." There was a slight hardening
in Em's eyes. She still wasn't fully convinced of Lucian's
death. It wasn't worth fighting over now, but Maeko
couldn't afford to doubt. "I never got a great look at him,
he was holding my wrists and stayed behind me, but if
you find Joel, I'm willing to bet you'll find him too."

Em nodded. "Well enough. I'm going to get this
arm properly seen to then head out of the city for a bit to
work up some of my contacts and see if I can get some
more help coming our way. This whole thing is getting
out of hand." She turned, took a few steps, then turned
back. Her gaze riveted on Maeko. "Good work, partner,

and tell your beau thanks for me." She spun and strode swiftly from the room.

"You're welcome," Chaff murmured to the fire.

Maeko turned her attention to eating. She was going to need her strength for the coming conversation.

"When you're strong enough, we'll head out to Whitechapel," Chaff stated.

Diggs cleared his throat, moved Macak to the floor and stood. "If you two are set, I'll be heading back out to check on the boys."

Chaff nodded. "Thanks, Mate."

"Of course." Diggs walked around the back of the settee and put a hand on Maeko's shoulder. "Go easy on him. He's fragile."

Chaff gave him a wry smirk.

She grinned. "I'll try. Thanks, Diggs."

He gave her shoulder a gentle squeeze and left the room. Perhaps he sensed what was about to come.

CHAPTER TWENTY ONE

Macak moved to her lap while she finished eating. It was hard to swallow the remains of the meal with Chaff looking on so expectantly. After forcing the last bites down, she set her bowl on the table and looked up at him. There was a certain anticipation behind his easy stance that made her uncomfortable.

Before she could decide her next course of action, she needed a little more information. Maybe it wouldn't be necessary to start a row with him. "What time is it?"

"About half-five."

"In the evening?"

He nodded.

She'd slept through the day then, but not quite long enough to force the decision. "Before we go to Whitechapel—"

"No." His eyes flashed and his jaw tightened, the relaxed posture vanishing. He had expected this and was ready for battle. The set of his jaw told her he didn't intend to let her win this time.

"Please hear me out."

"No."

There was more than one way to handle this. If the battle could not be won, then she would simply avoid it. She set Macak to one side and jumped to her feet.

Having to place a hand on the arm of the settee for balance when the room rocked around her wasn't part of the plan, but it steadied quickly enough. "I'm going."

He took a step toward her. "Where?"

"To Chelsea. I want to be sure that no one followed Ash back to my mum's house last night."

He threw his hands up in frustration. "Why can't you let other folk take care of themselves once in a while? You've nearly been killed twice in just a few days. Isn't that enough for you?"

And you've saved me both times, you and Diggs. She was asking a lot. Too much perhaps. She held his gaze. "It's my mum, Chaff."

The anger in his eyes broke, exposing a deeper pain that she almost couldn't bear to look at.

He walked up to her and brushed her hair back with his fingers. "I can't keep doing this, Mae. Maybe you don't realize how it kills me inside to think of something happening to you, and yet I have to face it over and over again because you insist on putting yourself in danger. Your mum's a capable woman. Let it go this time."

He drew her into his arms and she leaned into him, pressing her cheek against his chest, listening to his heartbeat. She was so tired and here was someone warm and strong and wanting to care for her. It would be so easy just to stay and let him hold her like this. Why not let the others take care of themselves this time and go with him?

Her stomach felt hollow despite the food. She couldn't let it go. Not knowing how the worry would nag at her until it drove them both mad.

She slid her arms around his waist. "Come with me," she murmured. His muscles tightened against her. If he wanted to, he was strong enough to make her stay, especially in her current condition, but he wouldn't do that to her. "As soon as I see they're all right, we'll go to Whitechapel. I promise."

She could feel his muscles gradually relax again. He kissed her head. "I must be moonstruck," he muttered.

She smiled, tightening her arms around him. "Thank you."

They let it get a little darker out before going to catch a hansom to Chelsea. It wasn't raining anymore, but a thick sticky fog had rolled out from the river, swallowing the city in a smelly murk. In the fading light, the fog looked like a grey-brown curtain hanging always a few feet in front of the cab. The front of the horse vanished in it, leaving a disembodied rump shifting ahead of them. It gave a surreal feel to the evening, as if they were the only two people in the world floating lost in a sea of mist. Maeko leaned on Chaff in the seat with Macak stretched across their legs. He put his arm around her, letting her rest against him. She closed her eyes, focusing on the contact and trying not to think of anything outside of that moment.

A few blocks away from the brothel, she leaned away a little to look at him. Worry filled his blue eyes, but he smiled, trying to appear optimistic for her sake. How had she not noticed the affection in his gaze before now?

"When did you realize you liked me more than... I mean..." She trailed off. How much did he like her exactly?

His shoulders shifted in a small shrug. "I guess I've known for a long time."

"Why didn't you ever say anything?"

"I was afraid."

She grinned and gave him a playful poke in the ribs. "You? Afraid of something?"

He took her hand and pinned it against his chest. Under her palm, she could feel the reassuring beat of his heart.

"Yes. I was terrified that telling you how I felt would drive you away if you didn't feel the same. I couldn't imagine anything worse than losing your friendship."

Her chest tightened. Did she mean that much to him? Was this really the same boy who always warned her not to become too attached to companions on the street? "What changed? What made you decide to risk it?"

"You showed up with Ash." His smile turned a little sad then. "I could see that he liked you, though he was far from the first to take interest. I didn't worry about it too much until I saw that you fancied him too. Then I realized the only thing that scared me worse than losing your friendship was losing you completely without you ever knowing how I felt."

Without allowing herself the time to question the impulse, she leaned in and kissed him, a soft, gentle kiss that stole the sadness from his smile. Then she curled up against him again, savoring the feel of his arm around her, and tried very hard not to think about Ash.

•

Things looked quiet when they pulled up a few houses down from her mother's place. Maeko started to get out of the hansom and Chaff touched her arm. She looked back at him.

"Should I wait here?"

Ash would probably prefer not to see him and the idea of being with both of them after everything that had happened between her and Chaff didn't make her feel especially at ease. It would cost them a little more to hold the hansom, but she still had enough of what she'd taken from Lucian's stash to cover it.

"Maybe that would be easier. I'll hurry."

He nodded and settled back in the seat, cradling Macak in his arms so the cat wouldn't try to follow.

She hurried to the house and knocked. Lottie opened the door, a flicker of relief in her eyes as she stepped aside to let Maeko in. Tomoe sat in a chair by one shuttered window working on mending a blanket. How she could appear so calm when so much was going on was beyond Maeko. Ash sat at the table watching Drake tinker inside a panel on his metal arm. He looked up and smiled when she entered.

Drake's dark eyes also shifted up to her, his expression neutral. "Good work last night. You did a great service for the Pirates."

She nodded to him. "Everything worked out as planned." They didn't need to know about the rest of the bollocks. If it went fine from their side, that was all she needed to know and definitely all they needed to know.

Ash stood. "I'm glad you made it. The airship will be here any minute. You can get out of here with us."

As if on cue, she heard the hiss of the airship drawing in air to descend. It was lowering down behind the house over the tiny yard. Drake's gaze on her grew more intense. She held his eyes, finding it easier than looking at Ash.

"I'm not going with you," she stated.

"What?"

She made herself look at Ash then. He looked confused and hurt. Guilt twisted in her chest. *I promised Chaff.* "I'm not going with you. I just wanted to make sure you made it back safe."

He shook his head. A lock of dark hair fell into his face and he swiped it back irritably. "I don't understand."

"Asher, will you go help them position the ship and take the sketches up when they're stable?" Ash held her gaze, ignoring Drake. "Now."

He scowled at Drake and grabbed the thick folder the man held out to him. When he had stormed out through the back door, Drake gave her a shrewd look.

"I thought we were working together now."

"I'm not a Pirate, Mr. Drake. I'm done trying to get myself killed over this."

"Just Drake." He closed the panel on his arm and latched it. Then he opened and closed the metal fist a couple of times before taking a few seconds to move each finger in turn. "The rest of last night didn't go so well."

She was aware that Tomoe had set down her work and was watching them. Lottie stood at the window, watching the street, one ear turned to them.

"Not so well, no."

"Where will you go?" He polished the metal panel with a soft cloth then tucked the cloth in his pocket.

"No offense intended, but I don't think you need to know that."

"None taken. I'd like it if you joined us. You have useful skills and I can offer you safe haven, but I can't force you, not in good conscience at least." He stood up from the table.

The back door swung open hard enough to slam into the wall then and they all started. Chaff stormed in, a struggling Macak pinned under one arm.

"Chaff?"

He met her eyes, a fearful warning in his gaze. "There are Lits moving in on the house. A lot of them."

Maeko went cold. She darted to the window next to Lottie and peered out through the slats. The fog was still thick. Drake stepped up next to her. Figures gradually appeared, only dark shapes at first, forming slowly into Literati officers with their weapons drawn and ready to fire. One carried a big gun like nothing Maeko had ever seen, the massive barrel aimed low at the front door of the house. Her heart skipped a beat when she saw the man behind that gun, his scarred countenance triggering a chill of fear. Hatchet-Face? Could they be crazy enough to give that murderer a weapon?

Drake sucked in a breath. "This is a raid. They'll shoot first and hope someone survives to answer questions later. Where's Ash?"

"I already warned him," Chaff answered. "He's up in the ship getting them ready to move out."

Drake gave him a suspicious onceover, but he nodded. "Let's go."

A shot fired. Lottie jerked next to Maeko then dropped like a ragdoll. Tomoe ran to her. There was a bloody hole in the side of her neck. She stared blankly up at them. Maeko stared back. A few inches over and she would be the one lying there.

"They're preparing to fire the big gun," Drake warned. Without waiting for a response, he turned and sprinted toward the back door.

Chaff pushed Macak into her arms, grabbed her shoulders and shoved her after Drake. "Run. I'll get your mum."

Maeko did as she was told, sprinting for the back door behind Drake. He raced through as the front of the house exploded with a deafening boom in a spray of splinters and smoke. The force of the explosion threw her through the open door. She landed in the dirt a few inches past the edge of the small porch. The world had gone silent. Drake grabbed her arm, helping her up. His lips were moving, but she couldn't hear him. When she was on her feet again, he grabbed the rope ladder and began climbing, motioning for her to come up after him.

Maeko turned around. Sound returned, the roar of flame reaching her ears seconds before she saw fire engulfing what remained of her mum's house. Her gut clenched. Two figures emerged from the smoke. Chaff supported her mother. Both wore a coating of soot and debris. Maeko ran forward to help escort Tomoe to the rope ladder. Once her mother was climbing, she turned to Chaff. Blood streamed from a gash above one eye.

"I'm done with this rubbish." He pointed at the ship. "Up there is our best way out of here, but once we hit land again, I'm having no more to do with any of this, regardless of what you do. Understood?"

Her throat felt too tight to speak so she settled for a nod. Finally, she had pushed him too far.

"Good. Get up there."

She turned and began to climb as fast as she could with Macak still under one arm. The ladder swayed with her awkward movement and that of her mother nearing the top above her. She was halfway up when the ship began to rise. She stopped climbing and looked down. Chaff leapt up, catching hold of the second rung from the bottom and swung his other hand up to grab for the next rung, making the ladder swing sickeningly. She wrapped one arm into the rungs, the other holding Macak tight, and hung on. Lits were coming out through the ruin of the house. One raised his gun and fired. A fine spray of blood flew from Chaffs hand where he gripped the ladder and she watched him fall, her heart dropping with him.

"Chaff!"

He hit the ground and the Lits closed in. Two men grabbed him, hauling him to his feet. He sagged back down to his knees, his bloody hand clutched to his chest, his face a twisted mask of agony. The ship rose faster now. For a few seconds, she considered letting go, but the fall was already too great. She turned her face away, clinging to the ladder and grinding her teeth against the tearing sensation within.

This is my fault.

"Mae! Come on. There's nothing you can do."

She climbed. At the top, Ash took Macak then grabbed her hand and hauled her in. She picked up the cat again, holding him tight against her to hide his leg from Drake's prying eyes, and moved away from Ash, walking to one of the windows to look down on the destruction below. The fog already hid everything from view except the rising of smoke, which showed as a slightly darker patch in the disappearing light. Ash's mum and brother were in the gondola, along with another man at the wheel who she hadn't met before. Tomoe sat in one of the chairs, hunched over and weeping. Perhaps she should comfort her mum, but the cold that rushed in to fill the fresh hollow within her wouldn't allow it.

Ash pulled up the ladder. There was blood on the bottom two rungs. Chaff's blood. A wave of nausea drained the color from her cheeks. He glanced up at her then grabbed a greasy cloth and wiped it away.

She turned to Drake. "I have to go to Whitechapel."

"I'm afraid we're heading the other direction."

She narrowed her eyes, nausea condensing and morphing into part of the unyielding ball of ice in her gut. "Perhaps you misunderstand. This isn't a request. You will take me to Whitechapel."

Drake took a menacing step closer, his expression darkening. Bits of debris clung in his hair. "Who do you think is in charge here?"

She glanced at Ash. It was his parent's airship after all.

He met her eyes for a second then turned to the man at the wheel. "Take us to Whitechapel."

The man nodded and began to adjust course.

"We haven't got time for this," Drake snapped.

Ash drew in a deep breath and faced him. "This isn't your ship."

CHAPTER TWENTY TWO

Maeko said nothing else until they neared Whitechapel. She stared out the window, unable to see anything other than the pain in Chaff's face when he knelt there amidst the closing Lits, his injured hand clutched to his chest. When they closed in above Whitechapel, the man behind the wheel, Captain Eli, who it turned out was a good friend of Ash's father, followed her directions with ease. He lowered them down over a park a few blocks away from the building she needed, managing to avoid obstacles despite the heavy fog and deepening darkness.

Macak curled round her shoulders and Ash insisted on coming with her when she climbed down. She didn't feel like arguing with either of them. Her feet touched ground again and she swayed, weakness from the prior night's trauma coming back strong. For a few minutes, she stood there, getting her balance and her bearings in the black night. When she closed her eyes, she could feel Chaff wrapped around her, his bare skin against hers, warming her. Tears stung her eyes and she snapped them open.

Ash nodded appreciation when he stepped down next to her. She didn't bother to tell him that she hadn't been waiting for him, but for her own abused body to stabilize. None of this was his fault.

She started through the soupy fog, one hand coming up to catch the end of Macak's twitching tail.

I'm nervous too, mate.

Gas lamps along the streets weren't visible outside of a few feet away, but she knew the route well enough. She and Chaff had moved operations to this low lodging house five different times in their years running the streets together.

A twisting pain rose in her chest at the thought of him and she crushed it down, storming across the street in an effort to outrun her memories. A block shy of the building she wanted, she held a hand back to Ash and stopped them both. She listened.

Sound could say a lot, especially when sight was so limited. She heard a horse-drawn buggy of some kind moving past slowly, wary in the poor visibility. A dog barked somewhere further away and, if she listened hard, she could still pick out the hum of the airship.

Cold crept in and she shivered, not recovered enough from her exposure in the river to withstand the chill in the air. Ash touched her shoulder and she stepped away, heading toward the building. She hoped he would assume she had been about to move and wasn't actually trying to avoid the contact, though that was exactly what she was doing. Down along the side of the building, she found the door she wanted and lifted on the handle, then shoved. It shifted with a reluctant groan and she entered, jamming it shut again behind Ash with a solid kick near the latch that made Macak dig in his claws. Avoiding Ash's eyes, she stepped past and continued into the dark interior, moving from memory.

This building hadn't suffered extensive damage like the one they'd left in Cheapside, though it had a few problems all the same. Mostly it smelled of mildew and damp and the rooms got cold in the winter. The street front portion was a shop owned by a man who took a share of the profits of anyone staying in the building. He also helped fence many items the boys staying there nicked and turned diseased squatters away, which made the deal equitable enough and gave them a place to stay with a legitimate façade.

When she reached the second story landing, she found a lanky, greasy looking youth leaning in the corner. He was busy cleaning his nails with a dagger.

He nodded recognition to her, his gaze lingering on Macak, then pointed to Ash with the dagger. "Who's the lout?"

She couldn't muster her usual defensive anger, though it would have been a welcome change about then. "He's square."

"Right." The boy grinned wryly and nodded again. "Where's Chaff? I thought 'e was comin' with ye."

She swallowed. "He got nicked." *It's my fault. I asked him to come. I couldn't let it go.*

The youth shook his head and went back to cleaning his nails. "Bloody shame. The boys put yer things in his room."

She said nothing else, afraid that the tempest of rage boiling up in response to his casual disinterest in Chaff's fate would lead to a fight she was in no condition to win. Instead, she continued into the building, assuming Ash would follow.

"They put your things in Chaff's room?" Ash asked in a low voice.

A faint guilt pressed in on top of her misery. She didn't answer. The door to Chaff's room was shut. She shoved it open and went in.

Macak hopped down from her shoulders and trotted over to sniff at his carrier. She opened it and glanced at the cat who turned tail and trotted to the opposite corner. She shut it again, letting him have his way. He trotted to the edge of the dresser and jumped up to her shoulders when she came in range. Even his slight weight was enough to make the pain flare up, but she gave his head a cursory scratch and bore it.

One of Chaff's jackets lay over the back of a chair in the corner. She walked over, picked it up, and pressed it to her cheek. The fabric was soft with wear. It smelled of him. A wonderful smell that made her chest ache and her throat tighten. She held the jacket against her chest and squeezed her eyes shut against the sting of tears.

I will get you back, she vowed silently. *I don't know how yet, but I will.*

"Mae."

The distress in Ash's tone sent a dagger of remorse through her and she cringed inwardly. She had forgotten that she wasn't alone for a moment.

She draped the jacket over one forearm and turned. The satchel Chaff had packed sat beside her things. She picked up her satchel and the carrying case and handed those to Ash. Chaff's satchel she picked up and carried herself. He would need those things when he joined them.

Ash followed her from the room without speaking. The boy at the top of the stairs, now picking his teeth with one freshly cleaned fingernail, nodded to her on the way out. She ignored him.

Down in the streets, she set a quick pace back toward the airship. As they hurried along, she caught the sound of footsteps on the wet ground not far behind them. She turned, taking them up and around the block. The footsteps followed. She angled back toward the airship again and slowed her pace, letting Ash move up beside her.

"We're being followed?" he asked in a low voice.

She nodded.

"How many?"

She listened for a moment and held up two fingers in front of her. They were almost to the airship now. She could hear it and their followers would hear it as well. The footsteps behind them sped up. Macak, responding to her unease, dug in his claws again. When they were close enough to see the ladder through the fog, their pursuers broke into a run.

Maeko and Ash both spun. He swung out with the carrying case and caught one Literati officer in the temple. Before she could do anything, Macak leapt from her shoulder into the second officer's face. The man threw up his hands, reeling in panic, and Maeko stuck her leg out. He fell over it and grabbed her shoulder, taking her down with him as Macak leapt clear. They hit the ground together and she twisted away. Soaring pain in her back fueled her anger. She kicked out, giving him a solid blow to the ribs with one foot.

Ash grabbed her arms, pulling her to her feet. The officer he'd struck was still down. Hers jumped to his feet and pulled his gun. Someone shoved them both to the side. A shot fired. She staggered, catching herself on her knees and looked up. Drake stood there, a smoking gun barrel protruded from a panel in his mechanical arm. The officer with the gun was on the ground again, lying still. The other officer, still down from Ash's strike, moaned and Drake turned the weapon on him.

Maeko leapt to her feet and stepped in between Drake's gun and the remaining officer.

Drake narrowed his eyes. "Get out of the way."

"No."

"This is war. You either kill your enemies or they will kill you."

"I don't care. I'm not letting you kill him." She stood her ground. It wasn't the first gun she had faced and it wasn't likely to be the last the way things were going.

Drake lowered his arm, but the weapon remained ready. "Daft girl, these are the people who shot Lottie and your street rat friend."

She didn't move. "Yes. Chaff's not even a part of this rubbish and you're giving them plenty of reasons to make things worse for him."

Macak jumped up on her shoulders then and Drake's gaze narrowed in on the armored leg, his eyes brightening with passionate interest. The gun barrel retracted into his false arm amidst a dancing of gears and a metal plate closed over it.

"Remarkable. I must examine that leg."

She let out the breath she didn't realize she'd been holding. "You can look at it, carefully, all you like when we're back on the airship, so long as you promise not to hurt this man."

He held up his hands in surrender. "Done."

She nodded to the ladder.

"You might at least take his gun away before he comes too enough to remember he has one." Drake turned away with that comment and began to climb the ladder.

Maeko backed up, keeping an eye on Drake while she crouched down to pull the gun out of the officer's holster. She handed it to Ash. The officer moaned again and she glanced back at his face, met his eyes and saw recognition there. She knew the young officer. Officer Wells. He wasn't a bad sort really, not like his partner.

She glanced at Ash then nodded to the ladder. "Take that stuff up. I'll be right there."

Ash didn't move. "I'm not leaving you alone with him."

She scowled at him. "Don't brass me off. I'm not in the mood."

"Stubborn bird." He grabbed the carrying case and satchel, stomped over to the ladder and began to climb.

Maeko walked over and picked up Chaff's jacket that she had dropped when the officer pulled her down. She took a moment to brush the dirt off. When Ash had made it a third of the way up the ladder, out of earshot, she crouched down next to Officer Wells. She shook his shoulder and he met her eyes, struggling to focus. He glanced at the cat peering at him from her shoulder and back to her, looking confused.

"You know who I am?"

His eyes unfocused then gradually focused again. He put a hand to his head, wincing. "Yes. Is there really a cat on your shoulder or was I hit that hard?"

"Yes, there is a cat on my shoulder." She scratched Macak's head. "You know I just saved your life?"

"Yes, but..." His eyes wandered toward where the other officer lay.

"I'm sorry. Everything happened too fast. I couldn't save him." That was true. She hadn't even known Drake was on the ground until he shoved her out of the way. Would she have tried to save the other man if she had known? Possibly not, given that she or Ash might be dead now if Drake hadn't come when he did.

Wells closed his eyes.

Ash was high enough now that he had vanished in the fog. She needed to follow soon. She touched the officer's shoulder again. "I need you to do something for me."

He opened his eyes, focusing a little faster this time. "What?"

"The Lits took someone earlier this evening in a raid on a house over in Chelsea. He's a street rat by the name of Chaff. He was shot in the hand when they caught him. I need you to find out where they take him. Can you do that?"

His eyes unfocused again, drifted closed. Blood streamed from the wound at his temple. She dug in his dead partner's pockets, finding a handkerchief that looked clean and pressed it to the wound. He flinched and gave her a suspicious look, but he didn't fight her when she took his hand and put it in place of hers over the wound.

"Why would I help you?"

"Because I saved your life tonight and because you aren't a bad bloke."

He drew in a heavy breath. "Did you help them kill Mr. Folesworth?"

"No." She took his other hand and pulled. He got the idea and let her help him to his feet. Her back screamed in protest. "If you want to find the real killer, perhaps you should take a closer look at his brother."

He spread his feet wide for balance and removed the handkerchief, gingerly touching the wound. After grimacing at the blood on his fingers, he pressed the handkerchief back in place and gave her a long, searching look. "I suppose I owe you one. How do I let you know what I find out?"

"Just find out where they take him. I'll find a way to contact you." She waited until he nodded then went to grab the other officer's gun. She looked at the dead man's face and shuddered, chilled by that empty expression. She glanced back at Wells. "Where's Tagmet?"

He looked down at the dead man and his jaw tightened. "They sent him to the new facility. I've been put on night patrol here training new recruits." He brought his feet closer together, gaining confidence in his balance. "You'd have liked it if that had been Tagmet, wouldn't you?"

Macak pressed his cheek to hers and she pressed back. "I don't think I would have liked it, but I might not have felt as bad."

Wells lowered his gaze and kicked the dirt. "Neither would I."

Maeko turned away and tucked the gun into Chaff's satchel, then she began to climb. Macak clung to her shoulders, crouching down and digging his nails in deeper the higher they climbed. She welcomed the pain. She deserved it for letting things get so out of control. Somehow or another, she would make it right. If that meant working with the Pirates then that's what she would do.

When she got to the top, someone plucked Macak off her shoulders and Ash grabbed one arm, helping her in. He took the satchel from her and set it with the other things, then glanced at the jacket on her arm and walked away leaving his mother and Sam to pull in the ladder. Maeko needed to talk to him, but now wasn't the time, not with all these people around. Besides, she didn't yet know what to say.

Drake sat in a chair with Macak on his lap. He already had the side panel of the leg armor open and was examining the inner workings with a delighted gleam in his eyes. Macak sat patiently, looking rather bored with the proceedings.

Maeko leaned close to Drake on her way past. "If you hurt him," she whispered, "I'll kill you in your sleep."

Drake sneered, not bothering to look away from the leg. "Pleasant girl."

She lingered a moment to scratch Macak's head then walked over to Tomoe who stood staring out one of the windows now into the foggy black night.

Tomoe glanced after Ash then looked at Maeko through red-rimmed eyes. She spoke in a hushed voice. "That boy, the one who didn't make it up to the airship, he is someone important to you?"

Maeko only nodded, afraid to speak. Aside from the possibility that her sorrow might break free, she also didn't want Ash listening to them, though the rumble of the engines made it unlikely he would hear anything they said.

Tomoe smiled and brushed at a pulled thread on the shoulder of Maeko's coat. "Perhaps I should sew some padding into your shoulders so that cat doesn't shred your skin."

Maeko managed a faint smile. It felt out of place on her lips. Tomoe dropped her hand. After a moment, Maeko took her mum's hand and held it. They stared out into the black night together, both mourning what they had lost that day.

CHAPTER TWENTY THREE

B y the time the airship started to descend again, Maeko was asleep in one of the chairs with Chaff's jacket draped over her shoulders and Macak curled contentedly in her lap. The change in the ship's motion and the noise it made when the engine cut back and they drew in air to descend snapped her awake. Tomoe, Samuel and Julia were asleep as well. Ash stood staring out a window toward the back of the gondola. Drake stood next to the captain, providing direction on where to land the ship.

Maeko slid her arms into the jacket. It didn't matter that it was too big. Then she picked up Macak and walked over beside Drake to look out one of the front windows. The fog that socked in the city was missing here and enough light came down through the thinner cloud cover to illuminate the large estate that spread beneath them, its grounds thick with stands of trees around big open fields. In the center, just ahead of the ship, was a large manor, not much less than a castle with a plethora of large outbuildings creating a wall around the main house courtyard all brightly lit and alive with activity in spite of the hour.

She gave Drake a questioning look. "Is this place yours?"

She meant it in jest, but he returned her gaze with

the utmost sincerity. "My family is old money. You could say I was the black sheep, but as the only surviving child I got everything when my parents died regardless of the family's disapproval."

She looked him over, noting for the first time that, for all the simplicity of his black attire, his clothing was of fine make and material. His wolfish look, emphasized by dark stubble and the greasy sheen of his overlong black hair, gave him the appearance of someone you'd be afraid to meet in a dark alley, not moneyed gentry.

"I have to admit, I'm a little... surprised."

He grinned, a disturbingly feral expression. "Most people are. I offered this place as a base for the Pirate efforts. I've also been developing technologies here to help us fight the Literati. With those drawings you appropriated, I can step up my development."

She smirked. "Appropriated. Funny how that word makes it seem so much more official. I nicked them."

"It all works out the same in the end, doesn't it?"

"I suppose so." She stared down at the vast holding, growing larger as they descended toward the courtyard in front of the main house. Several men came out into the courtyard and Ash dropped out lines for them to anchor the ship. "What do you plan to do now?"

"Now." He looked down at Macak nestled in her arms. After a minute, he met her eyes. He stepped closer and spoke in a hushed voice, though she couldn't figure who on the ship he might not want to overhear. "The Literati have started an experimental 'reform' program to remake violent criminals. They're taking these prisoners somewhere and we believe whatever they are doing there is related to the weapons development program that Clockwork Enterprises just announced. Forced labor perhaps. We also have reason to think they may have taken Captain Garrett there. He's a skilled engineer. They'd be fools not to put him to work on their weapons development. Now we focus on our own development while we try to verify where that program is set up and what they're working on there. Then we take them down."

She glanced at him. His nearness made her uneasy, but she refused to let him see that. "So how do we find out where the Lits are taking these prisoners?"

"Ideally, we would have a contact on the inside. Since we don't, we'll have to work harder at paying attention and hope for a lucky break."

How deep did she want to sink into this? Did it matter now? "Someone on the inside? Like a Literati officer?"

He gave her a measuring look, a new regard building in his scrutiny. "That would be ideal. Do you have someone in mind?"

"I might."

He gave her his wolfish grin again. "I knew I liked you for a reason."

She turned to glance out the window and caught Ash watching them in the reflection. She raised her voice a little. "Don't get attached. I'm not the type to stick around long."

Ash looked away.

Drake went down the ladder first, carrying the folder full of drawings with him. Maeko hurried after him, Macak clinging to her shoulders again. At the bottom, she watched him greet the men there with brotherly handshakes and brief exchanges. She looked around at the immaculate stables and manicured grounds, at all the people working to keep it that way. Most of them greeted Drake's arrival with a nod or a wave, which he returned without missing a one. The dark loner image he presented didn't appear to have much basis in reality.

Something didn't add up.

Ash was coming down the ladder now, glancing at her anxiously. Pretending not to notice, she walked over to Drake where he stood now talking to a couple of burly men who looked similar enough to be brothers.

"Excuse me?"

Drake looked at her, holding her gaze for a moment before he dismissed the two men. "Something's bothering you?"

She swept the grounds with a meaningful glance then met his eyes. "Why are *you* doing this?"

He gestured toward the big house with a tilt of his head. "Walk with me."

Drake started toward the manor.

She hesitated, glancing back at the airship. Tomoe and Ash were both on the ground now, watching her with uneasy looks and talking in hushed voices. Ash looked hopeful when she met his eyes. She turned and hurried after Drake.

"I'm doing this because the Literati movement is widening the gulf between the classes and turning the working class into little better than slaves to their wealthy counterparts. Too many people in power are Literati and they have the queen's ear. The only way to stop things from spiraling out of control is with a show of force that will leave them reeling. Then the people in power will have to acknowledge the other side."

A well-dressed gentleman opened the door for them, bowing to Drake.

Drake nodded to him. "Thank you, Edward."

Maeko murmured a quick thank you and followed him inside. She stopped there, taking in the elegant front entry. A sweeping staircase rose up on one side of the main room, the handrail carved to look like a thick winding vine that originated from a big ivory, blue and gold planter at the base of the stairs. The entry itself had a magnificent marble floor of swirling browns and creams. A life size marble statue of a rearing stallion stood in the center of the entry beneath a massive, glittering chandelier hung from a domed ceiling high above.

She stared up at the rearing horse for a time until she realized Drake was watching her with a smirk. When she looked at him, he started to walk again and she fell into step beside him.

"This is what I mean. All this wealth." She followed him around the statue toward a door under the curving staircase. "Shouldn't you be Literati?"

"Should I?" He glanced around the room with vague disinterest. "Perhaps. I never did get on well with the well-to-do. I spent my childhood seeking companionship among the family servants."

He opened the door for her and she walked ahead into a long hallway, plain and poorly lit compared to the entry. In fact, it looked as if no one even dusted back here. He opened the first door on the right and she stopped, staring down a flight of dimly lit stairs. At his gesture, she started down them, stroking Macak's tail where it curled around her neck for the faint reassurance it provided.

"My parents eventually gave up on making a gentleman out of me. Instead, they decided it best to stop taking me to their highbrow social events. At fourteen, I ran away. I went to work in a factory and spent my evenings carousing with the common blokes I worked with. I met a number of Pirates and came to realize that most of them were quite decent people with legitimate complaints. My parents, proud supporters of the Literati I might add, made a paltry attempt at locating me. They were disappointed when I returned home six months later. I decided then that I would never stand for the things they represented."

They went down a few flights and entered another hallway, this one walled in with brick and much darker and shorter than the last, ending in a big metal door.

"So you're doing all this to spite your family?"

He chuckled, finding it far more amusing than she did. "That and other such noble causes."

"Such as?"

"Power, influence, popularity. The usual misguided ambitions." He went through a quick series of turns on the dial alongside the door. A chorus of clicks and mechanical grumbling came from within the door, then it shifted open.

They entered a bright room several times larger than the entry and at least as tall. Five tables stood in one end of the room with several weapons and false limbs in various states of completion laid upon them amidst a cornucopia of gleaming metal parts and tools. Two men and one woman bent over separate tables, focused on their work. Each wore heavy leather gloves and rather complicated looking monocles for focusing on the more delicate details of their work. The nearest man, a burly bloke, had what looked like armor of leather and brass covering one arm from the shoulder down. The glove of the armor sported an array of delicate brass attachments he was using to work on the inside of what looked like a small cannon.

The woman held Maeko's attention for a moment. She looked out of place among the tools with her glossy red hair tied loose at the nape of her neck and her full lips pressed together in thought. Aside from a nose that was a little too narrow and prominent, she was the picture of feminine beauty. Her long slender fingers, however, handled the tools with dexterity born of familiarity, making it clear she felt at home with her work.

Past the tables was a wide-open space full of large curved metal pieces that Maeko imagined the ribs of a whale might look like. A much smaller man stood arranging these, checking to see if the ends matched up properly to a long bar in the center. Beyond that was another door, also metal and larger than the last. She could hear clanging, like the sound of many hammers working hot metal, from beyond the big door.

"The forges are through there," Drake offered.

"What are those?" She nodded to the long metal pieces.

Macak hopped down to the nearest table and sniffed at some of the parts before he commenced batting a screw around the smooth surface.

"Those, dear girl, are the bones of my battleship."

He was serious. This man meant to wage war against the Literati and he had the means to do so. No matter his motives, he could be a useful ally. At least until she got Chaff out of Literati hands, she would help him wage his war.

"Brilliant. But why are you showing it to me."

Drake smiled at her. "You've done us a great service and I believe you can be a valuable addition here, but I need your trust, which means I need to trust you."

It was an answer she could appreciate and she didn't doubt he knew it.

The two men and the woman who had been working at the tables had abandoned their work to gather around Macak. The cat pranced before them, his gleaming metal leg reflecting like starlight in their eyes. The big man crouched down, bringing his eyes even with the table to watch the appendage move.

The woman looked up at Drake and stepped around the table. She pulled off the monocle and flung her arms around him, kissing him with an intimacy that made Maeko flush and look away. Then she turned back to the table.

"Where'd you find this marvelous creature?"

"He comes to us courtesy of this marvelous young lady," Drake nodded to Maeko. "Along with these." He tossed the folder of sketches down on the table.

The woman opened it, long, elegant fingers flipping

through the first several pages. The two men leaned in to look and all three smiled like kids given a bucket of candy. They turned their excited eyes on Maeko after a moment and the woman held one hand out to her.

"Crimson Delevay," she offered.

Maeko took the hand. "Maeko. It's a pleasure to meet you."

Crimson smiled and wrapped both hands around Maeko's. She had smooth hands, tipped with long red nails, and a firm grip. "Oh no kitten, the pleasure is all mine. You have no idea what these things will do for us. How did you get them?"

She fought an urge to pull her hand away and go find a dark corner to hide in. Instead, she met Crimson's vibrant emerald eyes. "I nicked them. Same way any self-respecting street rat would."

The men laughed at that.

Crimson only smiled and stepped close to put one hand on her shoulder and the other against her cheek. "You're not a street rat now, love. You're a hero." She kissed Maeko on the other cheek.

Maeko flushed. *I think I'd rather be a street rat.*

Drake came to her rescue. "Don't overwhelm the girl."

Crimson released her and stepped back, batting her thick lashes at the wolfish man. "You're just jealous. Have you given her a room yet?"

"I was getting to that. Take a look through those sketches and see what we can do with them."

"I'd like to take a closer look at that leg too," the burly bloke stated, his eyes following Macak as the cat leapt back to Maeko's shoulders. The monocle made him look vaguely insectile.

Drake gave the cat a wry look. "You'll get a chance later."

When they arrived back in the entry, Tomoe, Ash, Julia, and Samuel were waiting near the statue. Tomoe and Ash watched them approach with matching looks of disapproval.

Drake leaned close and murmured, "I'd appreciate if you didn't say anything to them about what I showed you just yet."

She nodded. "I won't, but you should know Ash worked with his father on airships quite a bit. He might be useful."

"I'll take that under consideration." They stopped before the others. "Julia, I believe you and Samuel are already settled. There are a number of empty rooms upstairs in the west wing. The rest of you are welcome to make yourselves at home there. If any of you are willing to share, it would be appreciated. We have more people joining us all the time who are finding the unrest in the city not to their liking. I've business to handle, so I'll trust you can manage." He started to turn away, then hesitated and turned back to Maeko. "I'd like to speak more about your contact in the city. I'll send for you."

She nodded, feeling the eyes of the others burning into her.

With that, he left them. Tomoe, Julia and Samuel headed for the stairs. Maeko grabbed the two satchels someone had carried into the house. When she reached for the carrier, Ash stepped in and picked it up for her. She smiled uneasy thanks and started up the stairs.

The rooms were large and fully furnished. Julia sent Ash to room with his brother. He handed off Macak's carrying case to Tomoe and followed Samuel.

Julia stopped at the next room. She looked tired. Her long blond hair had started to pull out of its bun. "I hoped Garrett would have found us by now, but, seeing as he's still missing, there's room for one more in my room if either of you want, unless you'd like to room together."

Tomoe looked at Maeko. A sad smile whispered

across her lips. Perhaps this was a chance to rebuild some of that bridge.

"Thank you, Mrs. Harris, but I'd like to room with my mum. Besides, we'll find Captain Garrett soon."

Julia turned away without a word and ducked into the room.

Maeko followed Tomoe into the next room. It was done up in an array of lavender, pink and ivory fabrics with an elaborate floral wallpaper in the same soft palette. She never expected to stay in a room more lavish than the one Lucian let her use, but this room was splendid. The bed was a massive thing with heavy carved legs that ended in big wooden paws. An ornate wardrobe stood against one wall across from a matching vanity and two full-length mirrors were set into the wall. The high ceiling had gold scrollwork along curved edges and in the corners.

Macak leapt from her shoulders onto the vanity as she walked past. She took off Chaff's jacket and laid it on the bed.

Tomoe shut the door and paused with her hand on the knob. "Mae-chan. You must be careful. Mr. Drake is an ambitious man. He will take advantage of you."

Maeko faced her. "And I will take advantage of him. He can help me get what I want. I don't think it unreasonable to offer my assistance in return."

"And what do you want?"

Her throat tightened. She turned back to the bed, her fingers reaching out to brush the front of Chaff's jacket. "To fix what I've broken."

"Mae-chan."

"Can we talk about this tomorrow?"

Tomoe nodded and fell to preparing for bed.

Maeko slunk outside with Macak to give them both a much-needed break. Free of the manor, she stood and watched the cat explore the big garden. His vibrant curiosity eased some of the ache inside. Just when she was about to pick him up and head back to the room, Ash trotted up beside her, knocking her emotions into turmoil again.

"Mae, I'm glad I found you. I wanted to warn you to be careful around Drake, he'll..." He trailed off when she turned a frustrated glower on him.

"He'll what? Take advantage of me? Use me? I'm fully aware of his ambitions and the fact that he'll do whatever he thinks necessary to accomplish them. I don't need a lecture."

Ash didn't back down. If anything, he seemed to grow taller and he met her assault head on. "Don't you? Because it looks to me like you're throwing yourself out in the line of fire again."

The anger in his voice startled her. It was refreshing in a way, something other than frustration and sorrow, though she wasn't about to tell him that. "Maybe I am. If so, it's my problem, not yours."

"It *is* my problem! Like it or not, I care about you and I refuse to stand by while you try to get yourself killed."

He wasn't the first to say such things. She crossed her arms over her chest and spun away to stare into the darkness. "You saw how well that worked out for Chaff."

His tone softened and he put a comforting hand on her arm. "That wasn't your fault."

She knocked the hand away and turned on him again. "It *was* my fault, Ash. He asked me not to go, but I wouldn't listen. Instead, I talked him into coming with me. He shouldn't have even been there." She turned away again and wiped at a tear. Ash stood silent while she went to gather up Macak. She hugged the cat close and put her cheek against his soft head.

"Do you love Chaff?"

Her mouth went dry. "Yes." She swallowed. "No.

I don't know. It doesn't matter. What happened is my fault and I have to find a way to make it right."

"You said yes first. I suspect that's the more honest answer."

She couldn't argue with him. He wasn't wrong. She swallowed against the stinging in her throat. "I'm sorry, Ash. I didn't..." She trailed off, not sure what she meant to say. Nothing she said was going to make this easier for either of them.

He drew in a deep breath and exhaled. "Don't be. I'm not that fond of the bloke myself, but I can see that he means a lot to you. I'm not going to get all barmy about it. Can't say it doesn't hurt though."

She turned to look at him. He wouldn't meet her eyes. The hurt was plain on his face, but there was no pain-free way to handle this. "May not matter now anyway. I've lost him." Would Wells come through? Would Drake?

"You and I are still a team, right?"

"Sure."

His expression hardened. "Right?"

She smiled, though optimism evaded her. "Yes."

"Then we'll get Chaff and my father back together. I won't even try to kiss you while we're at it," he added with a wink.

Macak purred, warm and alive in her arms. A light sparked within her as she cradled the cat. A light that felt like hope, but it was so frail and tentative. Maybe it would get stronger if she believed in it. "Perhaps we will."

They parted ways then. Sleep came fast in the soft bed after the trials of the previous days. A sleep that held her captive through the next day, interrupted briefly when her mum insisted on her eating some dinner. Then she climbed back into bed only to be pulled out again well after dark by someone unexpected.

CHAPTER TWENTY FOUR

Maeko forced her way into the narrow space between several stacks of big crates, her mouth as dry as if she had been sucking on wool. Two Literati offices, Joel Jacard, and a couple of other toffs she hadn't gotten a good look at were walking around the crates. She tried to breath soft and quiet. She wasn't so tired anymore, but she was still much too sore for this kind of stealth operation.

How had she let herself to be talked into this? Oh yes, Drake had made it sound so simple.

Not less than an hour ago Crimson had snuck into the room Maeko shared with her mother and nudged her awake. She had put a finger to her full red lips and gestured for Maeko to follow. They'd crept down the hallway to a library full of books, at least half of which she probably didn't have enough education to read. Drake had been there, clean-shaven and dressed in a fine suit, his long black hair swept back under a coachman hat. She almost hadn't recognized him at first.

"Maeko, I have need of someone with your skills."

The comment made her uneasy. She had doubts about her decision to help him. A rich Pirate was an oxymoron and Drake's desire to help the Pirates, given his status, still didn't make sense to her, but she pushed her uncertainty away. She needed his help. How better to get it than to make him indebted to her?

"My skills don't come free," she'd answered.

Crimson had winked at her then. "You make him beg for it, kitten."

Drake gave Crimson a sour look. "We can discuss your price later. I had a shipment of parts on route to a warehouse in Billingsgate under an assumed name. That shipment was pulled off the train last night by Literati officers and moved somewhere. I believe, given the nature of the parts and where the shipment was intercepted, that the crates may have been taken to Clockwork Enterprises' primary receiving facility. I have another delivery to pick up tonight. I want you to come along. On the way, we'll drop you at the receiving facility. All I need you to do is sneak in and verify if the crates are there. Then make your way to the roof and wait for me. It's a simple reconnaissance mission. It shouldn't be hard for someone with your background."

It shouldn't have been hard, except there was more than only the night watchman on hand. Instead, a whole mess of blokes, at least one of whom had tried to kill her recently, were inspecting the crates she had come searching for. Drake told her how to identify the crates, an image of a diving raptor stamped on the sides. Finding them was the easy part. Getting out again was a different problem.

"Where were these materials supposed to go?"

Joel's voice made her shudder, a reaction that proved uncomfortable in the tight space between the crates.

"They were bound for a warehouse in Billingsgate. We haven't been able to track down the bloke whose name's on the papers. Can't even find an address for him."

"Splendid." That voice made her stomach turn. Thaddeus was with the group. It had to be Thaddeus. No matter what Joel said, she didn't believe that man was Lucian. "Let's look inside one and make sure everything is what it says it is. If so, we'll have a couple of coaches haul these things out to the new facility later this week."

Time to move.

She slid to one side, moving slow to avoid making too much noise. They began shifting the crate next to her and she took advantage of the noise they made to move a little faster. She drew in a breath of relief as soon as she slid free, but she didn't get to enjoy it long.

"I'm impressed."

The soft voice behind her made her jump. She spun.

"Most people I kill don't show up walkin' later. It's almost a shame I'll have to do it again."

The man lurking in the dark behind her smiled and turned the knife in his hand so it caught a glint of light from a gas lantern sitting on top of the crates. He had a deep scar across his nose that somehow substantiated the dangerous gleam in his baby blue eyes. She hadn't seen Bennett the night he *killed* her, but she didn't doubt that was who this man was. His presence had the same sinister anticipation, like a snake about to bite.

She stared at the blade and inched back. "I wouldn't mind so much if you didn't."

"Shall we get the boss's opinion?" He gestured with the knife for her to go ahead of him.

She considered running, but the gun he wore and the knowledge that she had to get away not only from him, but from the whole lot of them, discouraged the thought. Pulling Chaff's jacket tight around her for the false comfort it gave, she preceded him around the crates. Fear prickled up her spine knowing he could bury that dagger in her back at any moment. When they came into view of the others, Joel's face went crimson with rage and perhaps a bit of embarrassment given that he thought they'd executed her.

Folesworth stepped out of the shadows and gave both Joel and Bennett hard looks before turning to her. "Maeko."

She sneered. "Thaddeus."

"Such assumptions. It seems I underestimated the power of your thieving nature, stealing my cat and sketches and now breaking into my warehouse."

He looked irritated, but something crept up through his cool regard, something that looked like grudging admiration. It sparked a little hope, until Bennett's knife touched her cheek and she froze, terror forming a suffocating knot in her chest.

"Your mates tried to kill me," she glared at Joel.

"She'd like if I didn't kill her again." Bennett chuckled and slid the knife along her skin, moving it down toward her neck.

She jerked away.

Irritation dominated Folseworth's expression again, but no longer directed at her. "Let's have a talk."

His words caught her off guard. She blinked. "What?"

"I'd like a few answers before I decide what to do with you. Bennett, please come along. Joel, you can wrap things up here. I'll assume you can handle that simple task properly."

Joel glared at her and she gave him a nasty look in return. With Bennett's presence providing convincing incentive, she followed Thaddeus up a metal staircase to a sparsely furnished office. Through the windows, she could see the layout of the building better. She spotted the door she needed, the one that opened to the stairs that would take her to the roof. Too bad she couldn't get there now. How long would it be before Drake showed up? Would he abandon her if she weren't up there when he arrived? Did it even matter, given her current predicament?

Folesworth sat in a chair behind a scarred wood desk and gestured to another seat across from him. She lifted her chin and ignored the offer.

"Stand then, if it pleases you." He shrugged to show how little it mattered to him. "I suppose there isn't much point in trying to convince you I'm not who you think I am."

"I know who you are. You killed Lucian."

"I should let Bennett kill you. He could do it nice and slow while I watch to make sure you don't get up again this time."

"Why? What can I do to you now?"

"I think I have plenty of reason given what you've done already. You stole the cat, though I can't say I miss him much. I'd almost consider that a favor, but you also stole some very important schematics from me and," he tapped the desk hard in a small show of anger, "it's become clear that your friend, Detective Emeraude, also believes I'm not Lucian Folesworth. I imagine I have you to thank for that as well. I do believe we'll catch up with her soon enough, but I need to know who else you've been talking to?"

"You mean, who have I told that you murdered your twin brother and assumed his identity?"

Thaddeus kept his cool expectant gaze on her.

She considered for a moment. This was going to be one of those conversations that required careful handling. He wasn't going to believe that she'd told no one else. No matter what she said, there was a good chance she wouldn't get out of this alive, but she wasn't going to give him the names of people she cared about. She had to give him something. "A few Pirates."

"You expect me to believe that's all?"

"I would have spread it all over London by now, but people keep trying to kill me." She gave Bennett a cross look.

He winked back, grinning, and twirled the knife in his hand.

"What did you do with the schematics? Joel said they weren't on you when he and Bennett picked you up outside the Tower."

"Passed them off to the Pirates."

He glanced at Bennett. She made a point not to. It would rattle her nerves watching him play with his knife.

"Before I let Bennett have his way with you, tell me why you're here."

"The Pirates heard about some supplies that were taken off the train. They wanted me to find out what was in them." It was close enough to the truth.

"And then?"

"I'm supposed to report back to them."

"Where are they hiding out?"

She was ready for that question. "I'm supposed to meet one of them in town. I don't know where they're staying. They don't trust me that much yet."

His brow went up. "Yet?"

She bit her lip, encouraging him to think that she had said more than she intended.

His cruel smile gave her a chill. "Why protect them? If they had any concern for you, you wouldn't be in this mess now."

"They promised me safe haven if I did this for them."

"Is that all?" He sat forward and shifted some papers on the desk. He licked his lips. "What if I gave you the same promise in exchange for the location of the Pirate hideout?"

She shifted back from him. "Why would I trust you? You murdered your own brother."

Thaddaeus sat back in the chair again and crossed his arms, the smug victor. "Lucian wasn't the kind hearted soul you seem to think he was. His passing wasn't such a tragedy. Take the cat, for example. You don't think he got that clockwork leg to work right the first time, do you?"

The sick feeling in her gut started creeping in again. *Don't ask. Don't take the bait.* "What do you mean?"

"I mean, cats with missing legs aren't that easy to come by, but they're easy enough to make. Dear little Macak was his seventh attempt to get the design right."

Her stomach turned. She didn't need to hear that. The man had taken her into his home. Could he really have amputated cats' legs merely to test a new design? How could anyone torture and destroy another life in such a way. "The failures?"

"He dumped their bodies with the rest of the rubbish of course." Thaddeus looked satisfied with her disgust. "See, people aren't always what they seem. Help me and I will see that you are not only kept safe, but provided for as well."

"If I refuse?"

He nodded to Bennett.

Not much of a choice. "Did you kill Commissioner Henderson?"

His eyes flicked to Bennett, the motion so quick she almost missed it. "That's irrelevant."

A burning sense of vindication bolstered her. *I was right about the killer, Em, and about Thaddeus.* If only she could survive long enough to pass the information on. She took a step away from the creepy murderer and his eager smile. "I don't need you to provide for me. I can take care of myself."

"Name your price then?"

She chewed at her lip. What did she want that he could provide? *I had to be something he would believe was worth it to her.* Now that she thought about it, that wasn't so hard to figure out. "I've a friend who's been picked up by the Lits. Goes by the name of Chaff. I want him set free and I want us left alone. Promise me those things then I'll give you the Pirates and you can keep your secret."

A slow smile curved his lips. Victory sparkled in his eyes now. "Consider it a deal. Give me what I ask for and I will free your friend and forget you both exist."

She already had the information he wanted. All she had to do was speak a few simple words and she could save Chaff. Was it worth it? Could she trade Ash, Tomoe, and all the other people at Drake's estate to save Chaff and herself?

She shifted the jacket on her shoulders. It had grown heavier. "It's a deal."

"Splendid. You're a smarter girl than I gave you credit for. You're free to go then. You know how to find me. However..." he gave her a look of warning, "if you don't bring me the information within the next three days, the deal is off and I will give Bennett the order to dispatch you in whatever creative fashion most pleases him. And, for your friend Chaff's sake, don't try hiding."

No. Chaff.

She didn't give him time to change his mind. Instead, she gave a nod and hurried down the stairs, turning toward the exit. Going straight to the roof would provoke curiosity. When she was sure she was out of sight, she ducked into the shadows and began to make her way around to the door that would take her up to the roof. Her hands were shaking and her palms damp with sweat by the time she reached for the door handle. The last thing she'd expected when she saw Bennett there with his knife was to walk away with her life. She hadn't even heard him coming around the crates. He could move as silent as any thief she knew.

She stood by the door and counted to sixty in time to her rushing heartbeat, listening to the men moving around at the other end of the warehouse. They were covering the crates and getting ready to leave from the sound of it. She waited a while longer, listening as they talked. They were too far away now for her to make out any words. Their footsteps receded and a door screeched open. A few moments later, it shut with a heavy clang. She pulled the roof access door open while the echo of that sound still filled the room and slipped through.

It was dark, cold, and foggy on the roof. She pulled the jacket tight and hugged her arms around herself, breathing in the smell of Chaff on the material. Closing her eyes, she recalled the feel of his arms around her, warm and strong. She'd been away from him many times in her life. Never before had she felt his absence so much. Like a piece of her soul was missing.

Thaddaeus had made his offer. Could Drake do better?

She opened her eyes, glaring defiance at the dark sky. *I will get him back. Whatever it takes.*

THE END

ACKNOWLEDGEMENTS

The people who have been most supportive and helpful in this journey don't change often, so this page will stay much the same with a few exceptions. As always, there are many people in my life I'm leaving out here for brevity sake. All of you are still very important to me.

I want to offer specific thanks to the following people.

To my husband Michael for your ongoing support of my dreams and willingness to let me read you every book I write, and also for the wonderful photography that helped make this book cover happen.

To my mom Linda for your loving support and for helping me work out and refine my ideas.

To Rick and Ann for always being willing to read and give feedback on my books and for being the best of friends. Extra thanks to Ann for the beautiful jacket worn by the model on the cover.

To Kali for your spectacular content edits and for being such a pleasure to work with.

To my good friend and fellow author Eldritch Black for sharing long rides to the coffee shop full of cathartic rants and commiseration every Thursday and for being an amazing writing companion. Also to the rest of that writing group, you are all part of what makes my Thursdays so productive and fun.

To Aradia for knowing I would succeed from the first time we met and being an inspiration in your dedication to your own art.

To my cover artist, Raquel, and my interior designer, Brian, thank you both for your fantastic work and for your patience with me as I continue to learn this process.

I must also offer thanks to my sixth grade teacher, Mr. Johnson, for being so pleased and excited when I told you I was going to be an author and to my eighth grade algebra teacher, Mr. Siebenlist, for almost letting me flunk because you were so delighted that I was writing books in class rather than notes.

AUTHOR BIO

Nikki started writing her first novel at the age of 12, which she still has tucked in a briefcase in her home office. She now lives in the magnificent Pacific Northwest tending to her awesome husband, two sweet horses, two manipulative cats, and a crazy dog. She feeds her imagination by sitting on the ocean in her kayak gazing out across the never-ending water or hanging from a rope in a cave, embraced by darkness and the sound of dripping water. She finds peace through practicing iaido or shooting her longbow.

•

Thank you for taking time to read this novel. Please leave a review if you enjoyed it.

•

For more about me and my work visit me at
http://nikkimccormack.com.

•

OTHER NOVELS BY NIKKI MCCORMACK

The Girl and the Clockwork Cat
A young adult steampunk adventure.

Forbidden Things, Book One: Dissident
An epic, romantic fantasy.